THE LONG FIGHT

COMMANDER D. A. RAYNER was born in 1908, joined the R.N.V.R. as a Midshipman in 1925 and by 1939 had reached the rank of Lieutenant-Commander. At the beginning of the war he commanded trawlers that patrolled waters round the main fleet base of Scapa Flow. In 1943 he was given command of the destroyer *Shikari* and thus became the first R.N.V.R. officer in the history of the Navy to be appointed to command a destroyer. He survived the sinking of H.M.S. *Warwick* in 1943. He was decorated twice and mentioned in despatches.

Commander Rayner's novels include *The Enemy Below, The Long Fight, The Crippled Tanker* and *The Small Spark of Courage*.

D. A. RAYNER

The Long Fight

FONTANA/Collins

First published in 1958 by William Collins Sons & Co Ltd
First issued in Fontana Books 1978

Made and printed in Great Britain by
William Collins Sons & Co Ltd Glasgow

CONTENTS

A Royals
B T'Gallants
C Topsails
D { Foresail and
      Mainsail
E The Spanker
F Stu'n'sails

ACKNOWLEDGEMENT

This is a fictional story based on facts culled from the libraries of the Admiralty, The Royal United Service Institution, the files of the public Record Office, and substantiated by the models and drawings held in the Nautical Maritime Museum at Greenwich. To the librarians and custodians of those great institutions I tender my sincere thanks for the help they have given me in re-creating this piece of our history. And no less to Lord Hardinge of Penhurst to whom I am indebted for permission to retell this tale.

AUTHOR'S NOTE

So many years have passed since the *San Fiorenzo* fought
the *Piemontaise* that I am sure many readers will be glad
to have some information on the ships and weapons
before they embark on the tale itself. The frigate class
of ship came into general use early in the eighteenth
century in the three great navies of the time, the British,
French and Spanish. Originally they had been designed
to meet the call for a fast scout: a ship to carry messages
from the Commander-in-Chief to detached squadrons,
or to repeat signals from the Senior Officer to another
division of the same fleet which, sailing a mile or two
up or down wind from him, could not read flags that
were blowing directly towards them. The speed of a
fleet of line-of-battle ships was then, by our standards,
terribly slow and very rarely exceeded walking pace; for
not only was it reduced to that of the slowest ship, but
even then a margin had to be left for manoeuvring. The
frigate, sailing independently and built on finer lines
than her heavily armed sisters, could reckon to make
nearly double the speed of the fleet. As at first conceived
she carried her guns on a single gun-deck, below which
was one long deck clear for berthing her men. Beneath
this was the hold, the cable tier, and the magazines.
The early frigates had a small fo'c'sle forward and a
poop (or quarterdeck) aft, the former as a seaman-like
protection to the guns, and the latter as quarters for the
captain and commissioned officers; on these two decks
were mounted a few light guns – mainly swivels.

Once give the British Admiralty a deck, and they

will start to put guns on it. The swivels were soon replaced by long guns. But because all the officers from captain to master were paid by scale corresponding to the ship's 'rate' (the number of guns she carried), the Admiralty were unwilling to increase the officers' pay just because more guns had been given to the ship, and when assessing a frigate's rate they persisted in counting only the long guns on the main gun-deck. At least let it be said that we have a genius for retaining our national characteristics!

To pass from the quarterdeck to the fo'c'sle it was necessary to go down one of two ladders that led to the open gun-deck, and when this had been traversed, to climb by similar, but not quite so ornamental, ladders to the fo'c'sle. It was not long before someone thought of running a narrow gangway along the top of either gunwale to save the descent and climb, and someone else pointed out that if the gangway were made a little wider, then it too could carry guns – particularly if these should be the new carronades just being brought into service. The recoil of these carronades was taken, not on a wheeled carriage confined by a stout rope, but by rollers working in grooves. It is true that the effective range of the new weapon was a great deal less than that of the long gun, but it could throw a ball of twice the size, while the total weight was less than half that of the gun on the deck below.

	weight	range	charge of powder
18-pounder long gun on carriage	42 cwt.	2600 yds.	6-8 lbs.
32-pounder carronade on slides	17 cwt.	800 yds.	3 lbs.

The reduction in maximum range was severe, but the accuracy of any gun was then so low that the ships of the Royal Navy and of most foreign powers preferred to fight at point-blank range. Except when firing bow chasers at a retreating vessel, it was not usual to open

fire at ranges above three or four hundred yards, and
then the reduced range of the carronade was immaterial.
The carronade's shot was large, and the number of
splinters it caused proportionately great (splinters were
the main cause of wounds), while its lighter weight made
it an ideal gun to mount on an upper deck. Even so,
the Admiralty managed to keep well ahead of the
designers and shipwrights, and although the frigates
grew progressively larger as the century advanced (from
600 tons in 1720 to 1,200 and more tons at the turn of
the century), authority still persisted in over-gunning
them, so that all our frigates tended to be crank.

By the outbreak of war in 1793, the armament of a
typical frigate consisted of a number of 18-pounder
long guns on the gun-deck, and 32-pounder carronades
on the fo'c'sle, quarterdeck and gangways. But although
she still rated as a single decked ship, she was, to all
intents and purposes, a ship with two decks full of guns.

With increased gun power came increased responsi-
bilities, and this new type of warship was soon used as
a cruiser to prey on enemy shipping; while, to meet
her gun power, the old gun-brig, which had previously
been used to escort convoys of merchantmen and had
adequate force to deal with a privateer, was replaced by
one or more frigates. As a result, by the middle of the
century frigates were used both to attack and escort
convoys.

The change in the size of frigates between 1720 and
1820 is analogous with the change in the size and duties
of destroyers between 1905 and 1955. Where then did
the *San Fiorenzo* fit into this shifting scale of size? Fortunately we know quite a bit about her. She was built as
the *La Minerve* by the French in 1781 and fell into the
hands of the British along with the Corsican town of
San Fiorenzo in 1794. As we already had a *Minerva*

frigate her name was changed to that of the town where she had been taken. Her adversary in this tale, the *Piemontaise*, was launched just twenty years later.

The two ships were very similar in size of hull, the former of 1,032 tons, the latter of 1,093 tons; but whereas the newer ship carried fifty guns and 366 men, the elder mounted only thirty-eight guns and mustered 253 men. I have not been able to come by a plan of the *Piemontaise* but it seems reasonable to suppose that her additional twelve guns were mounted on the midship gangways – she was but a few feet longer – and that room for the additional men to sling their hammocks (or hammicoes) could have been found in the covered space thus formed. The lay reader may think, and he will be right, that we have here a battle between a ship of one and a half decks and a two decker. There are many instances where a ship of inferior force has met and defeated an enemy who carried more men and mounted more guns; but there is not, as far as I am aware, another instance where the battle was so prolonged, and certainly none where action was sought when sickness had reduced the crew by a third, or was continued when casualties had increased the disparity to half that of her opponent's complement.

BOOK ONE

ON GUARD

CHAPTER ONE

The wind, soon after it had struck, had shifted to the north and blown with an unyielding and steadily increasing frenzy. With her bow pointed north-west to make good the leeway, His Britannic Majesty's Frigate *San Fiorenzo* moved slowly to the west under her three close reefed topsails. In the afternoon she had rolled with abandon and to either side, but now that the real wind had come, she rolled with determination, and only to port – away from the wind. Mountains of water, laced with a netting of phosphorescent foam, swept remorselessly upon her, burst into spray against her wooden side and flung water that was almost a solid sheet across her.

A sheet of spray, split into fingers by the masts, assumed the appearance of a ghostly hand momentarily grasping. But, to the four men stationed at the wheel and to the group of officers on deck, it appeared as a tent of wetness, thrown over their heads without warning, which turned to wind-driven arrows that were personal enemies. They drove between neck and towel, crept between overlapped coat fronts and, at the slightest movement of their victim's body, became possessed of a devilish ingenuity to penetrate still farther into the defences.

Captain George Nicholas Hardinge, First Lieutenant

William Dawson and the sailing master, M. Dunnovan, stood together by the mizzen rigging. Spindrift rattled like shots against the bulky tarpaulin coats with the wide collars, and the pale gleam from the waves glinted on the wet curved crowns of the heavily varnished straw hats. The captain was distinguished only by reason of his slighter carriage, and that by comparison with the squat bulk of his two companions who waited with the patient strength of oxen on their master's commands.

So much spume was being blown across the ship that, although they had known rain to be falling when darkness closed in, none knew whether the water, which washed from side to side across the deck or blew about in little whirlwinds, was still mixed with rain or not. Hardinge had seen, from time to time, minute beads of phosphorescence in the shallow ripples. Fresh water, he knew, soon killed the power of the tiny marine creatures to emit their ghostly light. He guessed the rain had stopped – and that suggested even more wind. The remainder of those on deck were in some ways more fortunate than the three officers. They crouched beneath the weather rail between the guns. But there (and just because they were out of the wind) they were made more aware of the angle of the tall masts. It was not usual to be able to see the mastheads without tilting back the head, and so the sight of their masts' inclined length was more un-nerving for those in shelter than for the few who must stand upright against the wind's fury.

'. . . log,' Hardinge heard Dunnovan's shout. He nodded without turning round.

Five minutes later he was aware of the pressure of a body against his. 'Well?' he shouted as, still keeping his eyes on the waves, he bent his head to make shelter for them both with the brim of his hat.

'Three and a quarter through the water, sir. Not much more than two, on course.'

A heavier than usual sheet of water spread itself over the ship. The larger wave had a larger trough. She fell over farther than ever before – until her men caught their breath and wondered when she would come back. In rolling so long she raised her weather side, and for a moment the wind was prevented by the rail from tearing across the quarterdeck. In the sudden cessation of its attack there was easement, almost quiet.

And in that moment of comparative peace, which held such foreboding, the captain heard the bell struck eight times – Monday's midnight, and Ceylon two hundred miles ahead.

CHAPTER TWO

Dawn creeping after night, confirmed the captain's impression that the seas were higher than when darkness had fallen. If larger, they were less steep, but this easement was offset by the increase in the power of their heavy crests. Turning over in hoary curls they roared down the flank of the waves. When they struck the ship they thundered against the channel plates, which stood out four feet from the ship's side and carried the dead-eyes to which the lower end of the shrouds were fastened. Their blows shook her from end to end. Men felt as if each thrust was directed against their own bodies. The overcast sky was underhung with scurrying cloud wrack of darker grey. The lack of any rain was paradoxically depressing to their spirits. The sky looked full of rain. It ought to rain. That it could not do so was a measure of the storm's violence.

In these conditions it had been impossible to fix the ship's position by the sun. The master, chalking up the noon position on the slate, wrote with fingers wrinkled by continuous soaking in salt water: 'Tuesday 1st March, 1808. By dead reckoning Dondra Head bears west, a half north, 175 miles,' and, steadying himself against the violent motion, added the letters 'N.C.' meaning 'No change in the wind and sea.'

The masts and rigging were standing well to the weather. The reefed topsails, three narrow bands of sail, each half-way up its mast, had given no trouble. Familiarity with the gale's face hourly lessened its menace. The *San Fiorenzo* battled westwards, and as each wave was successfully overcome, Hardinge felt his judgement vindicated. With the ship held at an angle by the wind, a departing wave, high as the maintop, had a defeated appearance, and the captain could almost – but not quite – permit himself a derisive smile at the back of the retreating monster : a wave whose back had been smoothed by its passage under his ship.

A great fire seemingly burnt out may throw up little tongues of flame which, all the brighter for their short-lived loneliness, flicker in the dark. So conversation between tired men will be re-kindled, burn for a little while, and then for long periods die away. Hardinge, shifting cramped limbs, turned his head to speak to Dawson, who, as on the evening before, still stood beside his captain. 'It's not shifted by so much as a quarter of a point since it struck,' the captain said, referring to the wind. Speech had to be made between waves so big that the gale was felt distinctly less when the ship was in the troughs than when she had climbed the crests.

'That it hasn't,' the first lieutenant agreed grimly, his thoughts on the storm centre. 'No change means we're in the path of the storm.' He paused, while to steady themselves against a violent roll both men took firm hold of the pin-rail by which they stood. 'Bad it may be, sir, but not so bad we wouldn't wear her round to the other tack with her head to the eastward – that way we might still escape the vortex.' Dawson succeeded by his tone in turning what had started as a statement of fact into a question of intention.

'No. No, Mr Dawson, I'll not have that horse trotted out again. I said yesterday that it's not a question of seamanship. If we are to save the convoy, we've got to take the risk. We're making west all the time now. If we were to put her on the other tack we'd not lose hours but days. We've no idea when the merchantmen sailed from Bombay. Certainly they'll be at sea by now, and if there is a Frenchman on the coast . . .' There were necessary pauses in the conversation, and, because answers could not immediately be made, thoughts would often intrude to make discussion appear more disjointed than in fact it was. 'What if we do strain her and open up a seam or two? So long as the pumps will keep her afloat . . . What's this old frigate compared to three laden merchantmen?' Hardinge spoke with the sharp certainty of a young commander who is not really quite so sure of himself as he would have his hearer believe.

'Why in the hell didn't they send the *Terpsichore* to cover the ships from Bombay?' The words were only an emphatic question. It was not in Dawson's nature to grumble. 'She must have been in Galle since we left.'

'His Excellency probably reckoned that if one Frenchman had arrived a month early, the other could be there too. Then the ships from Calcutta would be in as much jeopardy as those from Bombay. Maitland is no fool. When he ordered our return he sent the *Terpsichore* up the east coast – and she is in a worse state than we are. Montague says his upper deck has got so full of rot that he'll have to land all his carronades next time he is in Madras for fear they'll fall through to the gun-deck! The Governor wasn't to know we'd hit this confounded gale, which is as much out of season as the French themselves.'

'And the only sound frigate that Sir Edward has left behind is way up north at Karachi. Properly caught with our breeches down – that's what we are, sir.'

'The *Pitt*? She'll not be back before the end of the month – only then if she finds a fair wind all the way south.'

'If only the fleet would get back from Sourabaya!' Dawson exclaimed.

'We'll not see them before the first week in April. Amphibious operations always take much longer than the Staff allows. Pellew is not to know that the Frog cruisers are already here.'

'The Ile de France, or Mauritius – call it what you will – must be getting pretty desperate for food.'

'Aye. And all the more danger to the merchant-men. There's nothing like a spell of half or one-third rations to make chaps want to fight – so be they reckon there's a good meal to be had for their trouble.'

'Pity we don't know which one it is,' Dawson said.

'The *Sémillante* is small beer compared to the *Piemontaise*.'

'If it should be the *Pie*, sir, she'll give us a grand fight.'

'Aye, and if we can nobble her, more honour too.'

The choice needed no further explanation, for both men were well aware that, for the last five years, the *Piemontaise* had been the terror of the coast and had so far eluded all attempts to bring her to action.

'Yes, sir, but if we were to be dismasted or severely hurt . . .' As the ship rose, the first lieutenant's words were lost in the booming of the gale. When the gust had passed – seen in its passage to leeward as a hissing carpet laid flat upon the waves – Dawson did not repeat his words. Implication had added strength, and the power of the wind that had hurled them away had been an underlining.

'At least we'll have daylight to see it coming.' Hardinge's thoughts had returned to the vortex.

'She's not as young as she was,' Dawson referred to the ship.

'Same age as myself. If my guess is right, we were launched the same month – that makes her twenty-seven in April. It's her starboard side that is the weaker. That's where Tyler and I had to plug the big hole before we could get her off the bottom of San Fiorenzo harbour.' Then after he'd watched another wave pass under his ship. 'We were both thirteen then,' Hardinge added.

'This way we'll have tried.' The first lieutenant had to shout the words to make himself heard. And then as the ship sank into the trough the captain answered more quietly, 'Either way a reputation can be lost.'

On Dawson's face, where the salt had rimed the unshaven stubble, there was an expression of admiration : the admiration that an older conscientious man who knows himself passed by in the race for promotion may feel towards the brilliant youngster whose star is rising. Aware what his own decision would in fact have been if he had had to solve the previous day's problem, he also knew what he would have wished it to have been.

'Here comes Surgeon Ward, sir.' Dawson drew his captain's attention to the squat figure, which – hatless and in shirt and trousers already soaked by the spray – was making its cautious way from hand-hold to hand-hold across the heaving deck.

The surgeon came to rest before the captain, with one hand taking firm hold of the pin-rail while using the other to brush the water from his eyes. Never one to overstate a case, he spoke seriously.

'It ain't any good, sir. In that atmosphere you can barely expect fit men to live, let alone those poor devils. There's a full seventy hammicoes slung at this moment, and scarce a man in 'em will be fit until he's had a spell up country.'

'One or two,' Hardinge thought. 'Even a dozen or a score – but seventy! One-third of my crew.'

The hot damp atmosphere, which was bearable in the open because the storm kept it moving, would, the captain knew, be stifling on the mess deck below hatches that were battened down and over bilges stirred to unusual stench by the violent washing of the bilge water. The use of the windsails, cones of canvas that normally directed air into the living spaces, was out of the question in that weather. If Hardinge's immediate fear for the ship had been reduced, his anxiety for her men was increased by Ward's visit to the quarterdeck.

King, the captain's personal servant, appeared hovering beside the two men. A short pippin of a man, he looked more like an ostler than the excellent sailor that he was. Hardinge had picked him up ten years before when he had first been promoted lieutenant and, the man following his master from ship to ship, they had been together ever since. It was a curious relationship, deeper in many ways than friendship. By this time both knew the frailties and foibles of the other so well that they had learnt to discount them and treasure only the good, and so it came to embrace more than a little of love.

In one hand King held a cloth that, like a sling, contained something large and circular. His legs were straddled across the deck, and, as the ship rolled, he bent one knee until the other almost touched the planks.

The captain, seeing him, said, 'Well?' querulously.

'Some porridge for you, sir. You must have summat to eat. You ain't had a bite since yesterday's dinner.' King's words were solicitous, but his voice held a note of authority, as if in matters of the body captains were in the charge of their servants. He glanced inquiringly at the doctor for support.

'King's right, sir. You can't go on without food,' Ward said. 'You, more than most.'

Taking the bowl and spoon, the captain favoured officer and man with a glance not quite so baleful as he had meant it to be.

'I wouldn't put it past the pair of you to have hatched this plot.' Then as the food warmed his stomach, 'My thanks all the same.'

Once its warmth had started to flow into him, hunger, which had been absent, returned. He ate swiftly, only pausing occasionally to look at the seas.

Dunnovan, the one-time merchant seaman, seeing his captain's attention fixed on the food, came up behind the first lieutenant. 'Well?' he asked.

Dawson shook his head. 'He's holding her on this tack.'

Dunnovan shrugged his broad shoulders. "Tis as I thought. Him being in the hurry he is, an' so young, an' new to the station, I didn't reckon he'd do anything but carry on this course until he's blowed off it. It's in his character, d'ye see.' The master moved forward cautiously, taking a few quick steps when the ship was upright and then pausing to snatch a hold.

King, clutching the curved cover of the companionway as the surgeon preceded him down the ladder, said, 'Worked a fair treat, sir.' The wind caught his words and whirled them away, and only Ward heard them.

Fascinated by the continuously racing seas Hardinge inspected each one. Dunnovan came stumbling back along the deck. For so experienced a seaman his careless hurry suggested the extreme of urgency. His hand, when not deflected by his floundering gait, pointed somewhere over the lee bow. His mouth opened and shut, as, in his agitation, he spoke long before there was any chance of his being heard. The words became audible. 'Captain, sir – Captain, sir – storm centre – wind'll – shift.'

Hardinge turned to follow the waving arm, but as he did so the ship sank into the trough and all he could see was the back of a great wave. Then they were going up, up, and the wind redoubled its fury. Following the direction of the master's arm he saw, low down against a horizon that was deeply notched by the receding wave tops, an area of tortured sky where frenzied clouds gyrated. Within the vortex the wind would lift, blow from all parts of the compass and from none for long; then, the centre past, the gale would steady to something more than its previous strength from exactly the opposite direction to that for which their sails were trimmed. The ship sank once more into a trough and for a moment the succeeding wave-back shut out the sight, but the captain had seen enough to be assured that the vortex would pass over his ship and there was nothing he could do about it but prepare to meet the emergency that rushed upon her.

'Have all hands piped on deck,' he shouted to the master and, turning, waved to Dawson who had found a waiting place by jamming himself against the bitts at the base of the mizzen.

As the disturbance approached, the eyes of the men on deck no longer watched the seas; their concentration was transferred to the crazy clouds which held the greatest danger. Men coming up from below paused irresolute, clutched some hand-hold and looked upwards. The sails, deprived of wind, slatted. The ship rolled as much to starboard as before she had rolled only to port, and the movement, thus suddenly doubled, caught many unawares. They slipped and slithered half across the deck, and then slid back again. The sea, released from the wind's hand, went mad. Pinnacles of water rose and fell on all sides without apparent cause.

The surface appeared to rush up the steep sides of the waves, and, when it reached the top, erupted into plumes of spray. When a wave had burst, it sank as quickly as it had grown and left a pock-mark in the sea centred by the stale spume of the crest.

Like a farmyard duck caught in a mill race the frigate was thrown in all directions, and just because she had lost her ability to queen it over the elements she had become, all at once, immensely small and impotent.

'Haul round the yards.' Hardinge's tone was urgent. 'There may yet be time before the wind's shift.'

It was easier to order than accomplish. In the violent motion every movement was doubly arduous. The yards on the mizzen, being the lightest, were the first round. The braces of the fore and main were cast off their pins on the port side, where a small number of men stood by to check them through the blocks as the larger parties on the starboard side tried desperately to haul round the heavier yards.

Before they had finished the wind was with them once more. A wave, monstrous beyond belief, rose on the port bow, its crest a foaming wall of water that moved forward. A thousand tons of ship went skyward. The new wind shrieked at them from the south-west. The foretopsail, caught aback, split once and then into a hundred slithers of canvas that wrapped themselves round the yard or quickly disintegrated into the hurricane.

The maintopsail, similarly caught by the wind, pressed the ship over to starboard – and farther yet. All the men who had been on the port side, sliding and clutching, joined those on the starboard. A welter of arms and legs between the guns was all that remained of the ordered parties. Almost on her side the ship still climbed the wave, As the crest hit, white foaming water swept across her. Then, with a jerk that nearly unshipped the masts, she fell down its back suddenly into the trough beyond and the roar of its departing grew less. But the fall, followed by the heavy crash, had imparted a swing to the yards on the main that the men had been unable to achieve. First the mainyard, weighing over two tons, then the maintopsail yard, began to move, ever faster and unchecked. The wind caught the maintopsail as the yards swung and by God's grace it filled on the new tack.

As one cause for disaster had gone, a new one was upon them. The mainyard, unless it could be brought under control, would go on swinging until it hit and carried away the back stays of the foretopmast. If they should be parted, then both the foretopmast and fore t'gallant mast would go by the board.

Hardinge, thrown to his knees and holding to a baluster of the barricade, saw the danger. Dunnovan, caught amongst a press of men who had been flung against the starboard rail, was equally impotent. Only Dawson, who had continued to favour a position by the base of the mizzen, had a chance to avert disaster. The end of the brace had been washed across the deck and now the rope was snaking through the big block bolted to the planks. The first lieutenant leapt to the companionway and using this to support himself, seized the rope and knotted it before it was wrenched from his hand. The three officers, each from his position, watched spellbound as the brace ran out, hoping against hope that the knot would jam in the block and that the block would not be torn clean out of the deck.

The knot ran into the jaws of the block. The rope hissed as the full strain came on. It held and the block held. The swinging mainyard came to rest. Men scrambled to their feet and in a few minutes the runaway horse was back in its shafts.

Without her foretopsail the ship was almost unmanageable. Desperately the four men at the wheel tried to prevent her head running up into the wind.

'Break out the mainstaysail. It'll ease her steering until we can get up the spare foretopsail.' Hardinge gave the order and then turned to be met by the carpenter's mate.

'Sir, Mr Carter said to tell you there was nigh on three foot of water in the well, sir. He's a-looking for the leak now.'

'Mr Dawson, have the pumps manned.'

'Aye aye, sir. Man the pumps.'

Soaked men taken without respite from bracing round the yards were put straight on to the pumps. Jerseys and trousers soaked by the spray clung to their bodies : strong bodies, fat or emaciated ones, were seen to appear almost naked as their owners bent with the pump handles. Because the pumps were of supreme import, every man aboard was conscious of the clankety-clank heard above the wail of the storm. The backs of the sixteen men on each handle rose and fell. Water, unnaturally clean, poured over the deck as each bucket on the chain tipped its load. Now because the need was obvious to all, the men worked willingly. Later, increasing weariness would cause exasperation, and that would lead to desperation and the feeling that nothing really mattered – not even their own lives nor the life of the ship.

Carter the carpenter hurried across the waist. The men at the pumps tried to intercept him with queries but he pushed on to make his report to the captain.

'A butt has started on the starboard side, sir. She must a' done it when she fell over that big one. The plank end's sprung out an inch or more. I've ripped away the inner ceiling and my mates is a-doing their best to caulk it, sir. But t'aint possible to make a proper job of it, not in this weather, an' on this tack 'tis well below the water.'

'It would,' the captain thought, 'be the starboard side!' To the carpenter he said, 'On this tack? Then it would be above water on the other.'

'Oh aye, sir. 'Twould be above water then – not that we could get a sheet of lead over it for a tingle until the sea has eased – but there wouldn't be a lot comin' in, not like it is now.'

The captain turned to Dawson. 'It'll mean a long spell of pumping.'

'You'll not put her on the other tack and raise the wound from the water, sir?' Surprise showed in the eyes he turned towards his captain.

'No, Mr Dawson. To put her on the other tack while we tingle a started butt would lose us twenty-four hours at least, maybe more. In all conscience the gale has delayed us enough as it is. Keep the pumps going. If, with their aid, I can keep her afloat, I'll pump her into Galle.'

Hardinge, closing the conversation, turned to face forward. He had no thought of a great decision made. Only within himself a small voice said 'I hope I'm right.'

CHAPTER THREE

Clank-clank. Clank-clank. All through the day the backs of the rows of men facing each other at the pump handles alternately bent and straightened. Those on one pushed down and bowed as those on the other raised arms and backs. They moved jerkily as marionettes, no more than a part of the pumps they served. Sixteen men on each of the two pumps, thirty-two men bowing to each other. With so many sick, each man pumped eight hours out of twenty-four, slept, ate, and worked the ship as well. The passing of the gale had left much to do, for almost every rope on board had in some measure suffered from chafe, and, even if it had not to be renewed entirely, at least fresh seizings were needed or another piece must be spliced in to replace that which had been damaged.

The men were worn out with fatigue, morose and sullen. They did not understand the urgent need to arrive at Galle and then press on to succour the convoy as soon as further information of the enemy's position or intention had been learnt. Beneath their breath they cursed captain and officers, and just softly enough to avoid being overheard by their petty officers, the boatswain and his mates, they cursed each other: 'Two hours hove-to on the other tack, and the carpenter an' his mates 'ud put a tingle over the bloody butt. There ain't no sense in carryin' on this road – with us a-busting of our bloody hearts.' But in two hours of daylight the French frigate could gobble up the convoy. Who knew? Who ever knew what went on beyond the rim of the uncertain sea? The Frenchman could have already struck. They might arrive in time.

The noon position on Wednesday had left only a little more than a hundred miles to go.

After blowing with increased violence for an hour either side of dawn, the wind had gradually eased. The sun had risen through a veil of tattered cloud and spindrift, and, even if its rays had been too weak to heat men's bodies, at least it had warmed their hearts.

Progressively during the day more sail had been made. The frigate's speed increased as wind and sea reduced to manageable proportions, until by four o'clock in the afternoon she was under all plain sail. Leaning into the wind she swooped over the seas, no longer a tortured ship but a living thing that drew her own life from that of her crew.

Clank-clank. Clank-clank. 'Land-ho!' 'Land-ho!'

The cry, arresting in its stark simplicity, froze all movement on the deck below, and salt-rimmed eyes were raised to search the western horizon.

'Pump, you bastards. Pump!' The boatswain, stowing between his teeth the silver 'call' that swung from a ribbon about his neck, laid fierce grip to the pump handle as he urged the men by the only method to which their tired bodies would respond – example. 'Maybe there is land, but you, you soldiers, won't set foot ashore unless you pumps.' Clank-clank. Clank-clank.

The officers stood in a silent group, as if unable to believe it true. The sun was setting in a welter of red-gold mist, and, as it neared the sinuous quilt of dark green waves, it silhouetted the land. First seen as an indistinct and smoke-grey shape the coast rapidly assumed a harder outline and a darker hue.

'Dondra Head,' the captain said. 'I'd recognize it anywhere.'

'Aye, 'tis Dondra, that it be.' The master and navigator confirmed the fact, more as an offering to companionship than from necessity.

'And Galle thirty miles beyond. I've driven the men and ship to make harbour tonight – but we'll not do it. Mr Dawson, I'll heave-to on the other tack and snug her down. At least we'll be able to go in as soon as we've light to see by tomorrow.' He paused. 'And Dawson . . .'

'Sir?'

'Have the carpenters go over the side as soon as she's eased.' And then, because relief brought weariness in its train, he was made aware of the fatigue that threatened to overwhelm him. Too tired even to ackowledge the salutes that were given as he turned, the captain made his way below.

The eyes of first lieutenant and master met. 'Well,' Dawson said, 'he made it.' A crooked smile twisted his lips. The statement was his apology for the previous doubt.

'Sure,' the Irishman answered, ''tis the luck of the devil the man has.'

CHAPTER FOUR

On the same Thursday morning that the *San Fiorenzo* anchored in Galle Roads, Captain Epron, commanding the French National frigate *Piemontaise*, snapped shut his telescope, tucked it under his arm and hurried across the deck to look down over the rail to where the ship's cutter was being brought alongside.

The ship, with mainyard backed, lay hove-to in the small glittering seas of the Indian Ocean, and because she was held steady by the wind she rolled but little and only rose and fell sedately as the waves from the north passed under her. Close beside her a dhow was moving to the southward, its two big triangular sails, which had been brailed up when she had stopped in answer to the frigate's warning gun, were now loosed as she turned down-wind to resume her southerly course. The ship's boat with the boarding party was returning, and Epron, no less curious than any other of the many men who lined the frigate's rail, waited with impatience to learn what report his first lieutenant would have to make.

Epron had sailed from the Ile de France on the 29th of December and had made a long, slow passage against head winds, to arrive off the western coast of India early in February. Life on the coast had been quiet — too quiet, for it was early yet for the convoys to be moving south. Even the circular storm that had hampered the return of the British frigate had spun its way into the Bay of Bengal and not made itself felt on the western seaboard.

In comparison with the many previous cruises he had made, Epron had now two extra concerns; the unusual number of men he had been asked to carry, and the state of the ship's bottom. As he watched the boat brought alongside he saw how the splash of the waves moved the long tendrils of weed that clung to the once smooth copper, and again muttered a curse on a Governor who had hurried him to sea without the usual chance to careen the ship on whose speed so much depended. But so far the foulness of her copper had had no effect on his success, for during the three weeks they had been on the coast, they had, until that morning, sighted nothing worthwhile.

Moving forward to the entry-port, Epron saw Moreau's head and shoulders appear above the line where the white of the deck met the blue of the sea. Climbing on deck, the officer saluted his captain.

'Well?' Epron asked, trying to discover from his first lieutenant's face and bearing whether anything of use had been learnt. The captain was a cheerful little man who laughed a great deal and this was in striking contrast to his gloomy pock-marked second-in-command. There had been a time when Epron had stood up to his strong-willed junior and the fights and disagreements had then been both long and bitter. Six years of serving in the same ship had ensured that either a working partnership would be formed or that one or the other would retire defeated. Moreau was now much more than first lieutenant, and Epron, who under a peppery exterior was inclined to laziness, was content that this should be so.

'Well?' Epron repeated as he stared into eyes whose blankness he suspected was assumed only to torment his own impatience.

'The captain was a rogue.'

'That is true of them all – but even a rogue has knowledge.'

'Of a sort – but who can rely on the word of such a man?'

'What did he say?' Epron, to control his impatience, raised and lowered himself on his toes.

'That he was bound from Bombay to the Maldives.'

'It is of no importance to where he sails. If he comes from Bombay he must have some news of interest.'

'If he is to be relied upon – the southbound convoy is soon to sail.'

'Soon – soon! Did he not know the date?' The captain's speech was eloquent of his natural impetuosity.

'He said within a day or so.'

'And the escort?'

'There was no frigate in Bombay when he cleared the port.'

'Does he know where the British ships are?'

'The *Terpsichore* is said to be on the Madras coast. The *San Fiorenzo* finished her refit in the dockyard and cleared from Bombay on the very day that we left Port Louis. He has not seen her since, but has heard that she has sailed for Rangoon. And the *Pitt* – the only one who is really strong enough to worry us – went north a month ago.'

'You found out a lot.'

'He was a very frightened man.' For the first time since he climbed aboard Moreau's face creased in a smile. His hand tapped the hilt of his sword.

'But this is wonderful news.'

'Captain, you should have let me burn him. He had copra for cargo and would have gone up like a torch.'

'And make an enemy of every native trader on the coast! You know how many hate the British.'

'He is a liar. They all lie.'

'Even when frightened?' The captain permitted himself the thrust.

'He will make for Colombo or Galle and sell the information.' Moreau turned the jibe aside by ignoring it.

'He will be too late. The merchantmen will be at sea by now. He would have to have done his reporting before this if his message were to save the convoy.' And then with a change in manner, 'Have the cutter hoisted in and pass the word for Monsieur le Paysan — I want a course for Cape Cormorin.'

'For Cape Cormorin?'

'The best place to catch merchantmen is at some point that we know they must round. I shall set up a patrol line off the Cape and wait for the convoy to come down to me.'

CHAPTER FIVE

In the great cabin that for a depth of twelve feet stretched across the whole width of the *San Fiorenzo*'s stern, three men sat round a table; and, for the reason that they had talked themselves out, they sat without speaking.

Hardinge pushed back his chair sharply. The zip of its feet on the black and white squared canvas carpet broke the silence: the sudden movement was both a gesture of his impatience to reach a decision and a symptom of his irresolution. The two officers that sat with him raised their eyes expectantly from a study of the blue plush of the table cloth. The captain, still in doubt, rested his hands on the arms of the chair and turned his head to gaze through the stern windows at the mud-walled fortress of Galle. Over the band of cinnamon he could see the red roofs of the houses and they, in their turn, were topped by the round-headed palm trees. Idly his eyes followed the dark ruffle on the blue water as the wind hurried towards the land, where, in contrast to the stillness with which the sun drenched the buildings, the trees were kept in constant motion and changed from dark to light green as each flurry caught their fronds. 'I think we have no alternative.' He spoke slowly as he allowed his eyes to follow the gyrations of a kite that, on brown and outstretched wings, tobogganed in great circles down the sky above the town.

'We shall be better off without them.' Surgeon Ward's voice had, through continuous repetition of his plaint, lost much of the force he had first brought to his argument.

'But how are we going to fight the ship?' Dawson raised the question without any anticipation of a direct answer, so that it became merely a restatement of a previously made contention.

'Time enough for that when we have to.' Hardinge shifted his eyes from contemplation of the distant fort to study the bars of the windows. The uprights sloped inwards, the angle of the slope becoming more pronounced as the frames neared the ship's side, and, because of the many different angles and curves, they formed a fitting subject on which the eye could dwell while the mind was in reverie.

The sound of the ship's bell filtered into the silent cabin. Hardinge rose to his feet and leant against one of the 18-pounder guns which, turned fore and aft and lashed to the deck, took up much of the space on either side of the cabin. The two other men moved their chairs back from the table and waited expectantly for the final decision.

'Dawson,' Hardinge said, 'have the launch put in the water. I'll take Ward's advice and land them all.'

'All seventy-seven, sir?'

'As many as the surgeon thinks we should put ashore. It's useless to take sick men to sea. The ship will be happier without them.'

'Our men look upon going to hospital as a death warrant,' Dawson reminded him.

'Ach, it's not as bad as that,' Ward said. 'Better than the berth deck.'

'We'll have them ashore anyway.' Hardinge's voice was hardened by a decision that went much against the grain. 'And, Mr Dawson, have my gig alongside at seven bells. I've to dine with the Governor at noon.'

On Thursday morning the *San Fiorenzo* had come to a single anchor off the fort at Galle : smartly enough, for even though she was old and short-handed, that was no justification in the eyes of her officers or men for a slovenly approach. During the morning the sick men were landed, and in the afternoon a boat was sent to *Hindustan,* only to find that before she left for Far Eastern water, the ships of the Admiral's squadron had already denuded her of men, and only three could possibly be impressed by even the most desperate frigate. At three in the afternoon the captain had returned from his visit to the Governor, and by the time that the men were eating their evening meal it was known throughout the ship that no more had been heard either of the convoy from the northward or of the French frigate which had so unexpectedly been reported off the coast.

On the berth deck the light was dim, for the only direct daylight came down through the two big hatches and was filtered by the gratings that covered them. It is true that between the mess tables there were, cut in the ship's side, small portholes some six inches in diameter. But as these had no glass and were closed by the simple expedient of inserting a tapered plug, they were little better than vents for the circulation of air. Each 'broadside mess' had its own table and benches, secured at one end to the ship's side and supported at the other by iron legs that fitted into sockets in the deck. Above the end of each table was fastened a set of racks for utensils, and between each pair of tables and forms there stood a wooden spit-kid bound with copper bands.

On this deck, some thirty-eight feet wide and a hundred feet long, and where the headroom below the beams was only five feet, there lived upwards of two hundred men. When the tables were down there was a space of twelve feet wide along the centre, but this was cluttered up between the mizzen and mainmasts by the hatch of the cable tier, and between the main and foremast by the big hatch that led down into the hold where the water and beer casks were stowed. At the forward end of the deck were the sailroom, boatswain's store and the powder-filling room above the magazine. At the other end, abaft the mizzen, there was a bulkhead, and beyond this on either side a short row of cabins for officers, with the gunroom at the extreme after end. Beside the mainmast four large wooden trunks passed through the deck, containing the chain pumps that once in each watch were used to empty the bilge. Then the clanking rumbling of the buckets as they swung against the trunks would fill the mess deck with sound.

Few men were so short that they could move about this space without bending their heads to pass below the beams of the deck above; and although there was, between the deck beams, almost a foot more headroom, the passerby must still remain bent, for it was here that the various messes hung their bags of potatoes, fruit and bread, while the usual selection of musical instruments, straw hats and personal oddments hung on nails or were jammed into shelves made of wood filched from the carpenters. And at night, when the hammicoes were slung, there was even less space to move in. Each mess owned an area ten feet long and nineteen feet (half the ship's beam) in depth. There was then only just enough room to sling the ten hammicoes and leave a narrow centre passageway.

The main impression was one of immense strength and massive solidity. Through this space passed the vast bulk of the three masts; the beams above were twelve inches deep, the coamings of the hatchways six inches thick, while the gratings were made of slats two inches square and very different from the 'tiddly' work fitted to yachts. Huge hanging knees supported the deck beams on either side of the mast and these, softening the corner between the ship's side and the deck above, gave the place the appearance of a low-roofed cavern.

The senior hand in each mess, either a captain of a gun or captain of a 'top', ruled a very mixed crowd of men. Those who had 'volunteered' were about equal in number with those who had been 'pressed'. If the latter had been gathered from all walks of civilian life, those who had volunteered had joined for the chance of prize-money, choosing the captain they would serve as carefully as ever their successors would one day study the form of a football team.

Lancarrow, a gun-captain and the senior hand of number four mess, was a volunteer from Plymouth. At thirty-seven he was one of the oldest seamen in the ship where the average age was nearer twenty than thirty. Three of his nine men were sick ashore, and of the remainder three were pressed men, two were seamen volunteers, and the last was one of those who had been pressed that day from the *Hindustan*.

Lancarrow was speaking. 'Well, if we're short-handed, at least we've got more room to spread ourselves. Cor, when I thinks of the number of men as 'ave sat at this table in the six years since we left Plymouth; we must have put ashore nigh forty men from this mess alone. That clerk fellow, Milne, was telling me we'd used up enough men to commission her five times over. Nearly lost a whole crew every year through sickness.'

'What they go sick of?' It was the new man, John Beer, who spoke. 'Sea boils, an' scurvy?'

'No – we ain't at sea long enough on this coast. Plenty of fruit too. You can't beat fruit for boils – lemons that is.' Lancarrow paused to push into his mouth a forkful of duff stuffed with salt pork. 'Lemons is good – limes no bloody good at all. There weren't no scurvy while we had good lemon juice from Malta and Sicily. Then what happens? Soon as the war starts we lose the lemons from Malta, and the Sicilians puts the price up. An' the Admiralty bein' what they are won't pay the extra, so they buys lime juice from Montserrat in the West Indies 'cos it's cheaper, but it ain't so good – not by a long shot it ain't. An' we all gets scurvy again.'

'You can get scurvy in London too.'

'Aye maybe – but you won't get it in the country, where people lives proper.'

'Then what is it that sends so many men off sick?'

'Malaria o' course. Lying in these festering ports. Take a boat inshore at night, and blessed if you ain't half-dead within a week.'

'Your captain seems a decent sort.'

'Oh, 'im – he's man enough. He'll get better as he grows older – they all do. Can't put an old 'ead on young shoulders, you know.'

'Does he flog much?'

'Only when the Irish goes mad wi' drink. We've a lot o' Irish aboard. Don't understand it meself – seems that every now and then they have a riot in the "old country" and the half that gets beat has to leave. Next time the other chap gets beat – and they leave. But the queerest thing is that whichever side they was on at 'ome they're as thick as thieves when they get aboard here.'

'They're always troublesome.'

'They fight damn' well, and they're good enough messmates except when they've had a run ashore and been to the toddy shop. Then they 'as to be flogged back to sense. Eh! What's that?'

The long trill of the boatswain's call echoed through the mess deck. Men stiffened to immobility and ceased to speak as they waited for the shouted order which would follow the pipe.

'All hands on deck. All hands on deck.' In the sudden silence each word was a heartbeat. 'Hoist in and stow the boats. Prepare ship for sea. All hands on deck . . .' The boatswain's mate was moving along the waist of the ship calling as he went. The words came just as clear, but less loud . . . 'All hands on deck. Hoist in and stow the boats. Prepare ship for sea. All hands . . .' The voice was drowned by the scuffling of many feet.

'Here we go,' Lancarrow said as he rose. 'Gor' blimey! Call this 'ere hooker *San Fiorenzo*? His Majesty's Frigate *Perpetual Bloody Motion* that's what she be.'

CHAPTER SIX

A few minutes before midnight on Saturday the 5th of March, Lieutenant de Vaisseau Schoy, Gunnery Officer and for the time being Officer of the Watch of the *Piemontaise*, leant over the rail and gazed up the bright path that the setting moon laid upon the ocean. Then, jolted to sudden awareness that the sea over which he looked was no longer as empty as it had been, his reverie was broken. The moon's disc lipping the horizon silhouetted three small black dots. With an audible intake of breath he stood upright. 'Ensign. Here – quick. Report to the captain that the convoy is five miles on the port quarter.'

The long-awaited sight brought its own problems. By the time Epron and Moreau were on deck, only a little of the moon's disc was still visible, and a few minutes later even that had gone. Epron, his short figure inclined to paunchiness, raised his eyes to speak to the tall thin first lieutenant – although, with only the starlight left, the upward glance was pure habit.

'What do you advise, my friend?' Epron asked.

'It is a great pity that the moon has set – otherwise . . .'

'Even if it had not, a night attack is a chancy affair.'

'It will be better left until the dawn. We know their destination and their course. Here the wind is sure to hold northerly for the next month, so we need not worry that it will change before we catch them.'

'It will be a blessing to get rid of some, if not all, of these lascars,' the captain said. 'I hate the way they squat on deck – you have no idea what they are doing.'

Moreau snorted. 'It will be more than a blessing. Myself, I shall hold a fiesta !'

'Alas, we have only salt fish !'

'We had fish for carnival too – and for Candlemas. God, how I hate fish.'

'Never mind – tomorrow we'll end our Lent a month early. They do themselves well, those Indiamen, they'll have fresh meat aboard. Does a nice steak whet your fancy?'

'Three fat prizes and riddance from these lascars would do it more good.'

'Never fear, my friend, you shall have both. Only three sails were reported?'

'Only three, as we were told. There was no escort.'

'That dhow said that there wasn't a frigate in Bombay when she left.'

'And one could hardly have beat through our patrol line without being sighted.'

'Then, my good Moreau, we shall try the Governor's plan tomorrow – course south-east a half south during the night. At dawn we'll make all sail and set our stu'n'sails.'

Unseen by the sheep, the wolf settled down to wait until sunrise, keeping some six miles astern and to the east of the unsuspecting prey. By doing so, she would make her attack, not with the wind right astern where one sail would blankey another, but with the wind forty-five degrees on the quarter. At this angle the sailing ship could obtain the greatest power from Boreas.

CHAPTER SEVEN

Until sunrise on Sunday morning the 6th of March, Dawson's watch ran its usual disciplined pattern. As first lieutenant he had, by custom, the morning watch. Then the pumps flooded the dew-damp decks, and the crew, with trousers rolled knee-high, holy-stoned the planks till they would dry snow-white under the sun.

It was Dawson himself who made the sighting. Three distinct hardenings in the dawn mist which, near enough to lie within the circle of the horizon, could be seen from the deck. Night rising like the curtain of a theatre had disclosed them to the sharp-eyed first lieutenant. The sun, soon following, set them as objects of colour in a blue sea.

The three fine East Indiamen were keeping station as correctly as if they had been ships of the line. With the wind free, they rolled slightly, and out of unison with each other, as the small seas of the Indian Ocean were trampled under their bluff forefeet. Bound south before the northerly wind, they swept past the *San Fiorenzo* as, close hauled on the starboard tack, the frigate stood to the north-west. Hardinge, called on deck by Dawson, saw them pass almost within hailing distance, his multi-coloured silk dressing-gown blowing round his thin legs as he stood barefoot on the wet deck, under the refreshingly cool down draught from the tightly curved mizzen topsail.

Two hundred and fifty miles north-east of Colombo and sixty miles south of Cape Cormorin, the most southerly point of India; these were so obviously the three ships he had set out to protect that there was no need to use the semaphore whose poles the yeoman of signals had hopefully set in the capping of the gunwale. A wave to each ship in passing satisfied all, and the captain of the *San Fiorenzo* knew that had any suspicious sail been seen, a signal would have been made to him. Swiftly the three merchantmen passed on the first leg of their nine thousand mile voyage to England, and the hearts of the men on the *San Fiorenzo*, many of whom had not seen their homes for five, six or more years, went with them.

As well as wheat from the Punjab and rice from Orissa, the merchantmen carried many strange and precious wares: pepper, ivory and beeswax; rosewood for furniture and musket stocks, sandalwood for medicine; calicoes of Calicut and silks of Benares; coffee for London's burghers and ginger for their wives; oil of the lemon-grass for ladies' scents; products of the coco palms – copra, coconut oil, and coir for ropes of ships; spices – cardamom, capsicum and tumerick.

Half an hour later they were only seen as three small and still pyramids of white, almost hull down over the blue rim of the sea. Hardinge had gone below to finish his interrupted shave; and the signal rating, denied the use of his apparatus, was stowing it away with an expression of peevish disappointment.

'Sail ho! Sail ho!'

The alarm from the masthead echoed back and forth between the curved surface of the canvas cliffs that gleamed white in the early sunlight of the tropic morning. Towering above the extreme orderliness of the frigate's deck, the sublimely silent contours of her

sails gave to the cry the bell-like quality of a shout
made amongst mountains.

Every man working on the upper deck heard the
hail and paused. The hopeful faces of the swabbers,
drawing their lengths of ropeyard across the recently
holystoned decks, were raised. The eyes of the men
who polished the water-drops from the shining black
barrels of the guns were turned questioningly towards
their mates. Even the party who, under the orders
of the boatswain, were going round the white-painted
hammicoes to make sure that they had been correctly
stowed in the nettings, even this highly disciplined
party raised expectant faces to the masthead.

Every man in the ship knew the object of their
endeavour. All knew that a powerful French frigate
was loose on the trade routes, but, however much
their patriotism would be stirred should they be successful in meeting her, the thought which really
prompted the greedy exchange of their eyes was one
of prize money. No wonder that when a single hour's
dangerous work could result in a doubling of their
yearly pay the men raised anxious faces to the masthead.

'Sail ho. Sail ho.'

Disturbed by the look-out's hail Dawson jerked his
stocky figure to motion. He moved forward as far
as the balustered barricade at the forward end of the
quarterdeck. There, bending his head well back, he
gazed upward to where fifty feet before him and a
hundred and fifty above the deck, the look-out was
perched dizzily upon the gently swaying mast.

'Where – away?' The first lieutenant gave the ac-
customed answer. His lips formed the words slowly,
for they had a long way to go and were long drawn
out. His hands cupped his mouth without in any way

disturbing the set of the telescope tucked under his left arm. His head was sent back, and his legs in white trousers were spread athwartships to ease his body against the gentle motion.

'Four points on the starboard bow.'

For a moment Dawson hesitated. To send the midshipman of the watch or to go himself? Better himself, for the dispatch that had sent them to sea had clearly said 'three merchantmen', and this strange sail could be the enemy. He started to climb the mainmast. Near his fortieth year and just a little out of practice he succeeded in hiding both his age and the fact that first lieutenants did not spend as much time aloft as on the quarterdeck. Main shrouds and topmost shrouds climbed, he came to the rope ladder that led up the after side of the main t'gallantmast. Pausing for breath, he looked aloft into the interested face of Hawkins, the able seaman, who was perched on the royal yard twenty feet above him.

Standing on the topmast cap he shouted upwards, 'Can you still see her?'

'Aye aye, sir – plain as a daisy.'

Holding on with one hand to the taut t'gallant halyard and shading his eyes with the other, Dawson followed the man's arm.

'You'll likely see her from there, sir,' Hawkins advised him.

'Aye. I can see her. A big ship too.'

There was no question of a mistake. This was not a couple of dhows appearing as one large vessel. The three masts could be seen and the recognizable shapes of her squaresails.

'You'll be expecting to be relieved,' the first lieutenant shouted. 'I'll send a man up as soon as I'm down.'

'Thank'ye, sir, thank'ye.'

For a moment Dawson paused; his eye, travelling over the rigging from an angle infrequently seen, found nothing that immediately needed attention. Below him the ship looked unbelievably small, as if she were entirely divorced from this strange world that was made up of great arcs of canvas, taut rigging at which the wind plucked until it throbbed with the low notes of a harp, and yards whose jeers and parrals chattered as they swayed. Up there the whole world seemed alive with constrained motion as the arched planes harnessed the power of the wind to drive the hull through the water.

A minute later Dawson was jumping from the topsail halyard rack to the deck. The midshipman of the watch waited his arrival.

'I'm reporting to the captain,' the first lieutenant said, and hurried to the companionway that led to the after-flat.

Hardinge was drying his face on a towel when Dawson's knock fell on his cabin door.

'Come in,' he called, turning, towel in hand, towards the door.

'Ship, four points on the starboard bow, sir. Steering the same course as the convoy.'

'Tack ship, if you please, Mr Dawson.' Hardinge had no hesitation in giving the order. Any sail near the convoy was suspicious and must at once be investigater. 'Have you called the hands?'

'No, sir. Not yet.'

'Then please do. I'll be up directly.'

For a moment when the door had closed the captain stood and considered the problem of Dawson. Three years before, the *San Fiorenzo* had fought the French frigate *Psyché* until she had been forced to strike. Lambert, who had been her captain then, had won his well deserved promotion to command a line of battle ship, and it could have been supposed that his first lieutenant – the same William Dawson – might reasonably expect, on that foreign station, to be given command of the ship that he had helped to fight to victory. But it had not worked out that way. It was, Hardinge thought, still possible that one day promotion might be thrust upon Dawson, it seemed inconceivable that he should ever seek it out. The captain was sure that if his first lieutenant had been asked the direct question, 'What should we do?' he would have answered correctly. Putting himself in Dawson's place he knew that he would have piped 'both watches' before reporting to his captain, thus saving minutes that, in certain circumstances, could be vital.

No rope dare snarl in a block, no anchor go down foul under the first lieutenant's watchful eye, but the *San Fiorenzo*'s captain did wish that Dawson had piped the hands before reporting the sail. Throwing on his coat and seizing his cocked hat, he hurried on deck.

CHAPTER EIGHT

Epron, his eyes shining with anticipation, stood by the kicking wheel and watched the white pyramid of his ship doubled in size as, with gallic gesture and arab ejaculation, his enlarged crew sheeted home the auxiliary sails. As each was set he felt the speed of his ship increase beneath his feet. The wind was fair, the weather excellent and the unprotected convoy had been discovered just where long practice had suggested they would be. His tactics had been exemplary and his humour matched events.

Even Moreau, hunch-backed and lanky, moved amongst the throng with a less saturnine gait than usual. If, in his anticipation, he dwelt more on the coming release from the lascars that the Governor had put aboard for prize-crews, his confidence in their departure was as great as his captain's sureness that the ships ahead would be taken. He even found it possible to be civil to Schoy, the precise little gunnery officer whom normally he detested. The owner of the eyes that had sighted the merchantmen and relieved the tension under which they had lived for so long was not that morning to be disparaged. Overcrowding had indeed made the strain almost intolerable. Very soon now he would be able to forget the ever-present problem of lavatories and cooking for an extra two hundred men. With success, discipline would return to normal, and with release from the lascars the continual bickering and fighting would end. Coming across Schoy as the latter was inspecting his guns he gave him a pleasant

'Good morning.' And, 'When you are ready I'd like the guns run out on the port side to give the ship a list. She'll sail the better for it.'

And Schoy, accepting the first lieutenant's order gracefully, did not – as on previous days he would have – suggest that such an order should more properly be given him by the captain.

Moreau, making his way aft, punctiliously reported to Epron the order he had given to Schoy. The captain's white teeth flashed in his sunburnt face. It was, he thought, on such occasions that his first lieutenant showed to best advantage. 'It is only a pity,' he said, 'that our paintwork is so poor.'

'Our guns are good enough.'

'True, my friend, but I prefer my ship to look as smart as she is.'

'It's easy to be smart if you spend your days swinging to a cable in Brest or Toulon. There's not a frigate in the National Navy that does more sea time than we.'

'At least the Minister of Marine might send out some paint,' Epron grumbled.

'If he did, the British cruisers would only snap it up – as they took the last shipment of clothing.'

'There'll be paint and to spare aboard the Indiamen.'

'And clothes too,' Moreau chuckled.

'Must I remind you, my friend, that looting is forbidden.' The captain joined in the laugh.

'But precious difficult to stop !'

Everything was going so well that the cry from the masthead – '*Voici une voile*' – caused something approaching consternation on the deck below. Without a word from Epron, Moreau was up the rigging like a cat, and very soon down again.

'The *San Fiorenzo* close hauled on the starboard tack. That fool Pierre should have seen her before. A league north of the convoy, and about the same distance beyond. I have left instructions to watch her, and to hail us if she tacks.'

'You are certain she is the *San Fiorenzo*?' Epron's voice was as blank as his face.

'Absolutely. Did I not see her for long enough when she chased us last August? Her lower yards are rather longer, and her upper yards shorter, than is usual for a Britisher.'

Epron chewed at his upper lip. It was a habit when he was lost in thought.

'She is very old, and has twelve guns less – these waters are cruel to the old ones. Even so we shall do better to proceed with guile rather than to risk damage by thrusting our way through to the merchantmen by force. For any reduction in our power to sail may lose us the convoy.' Then Epron began to swear, for the more he thought, the more he realized that by her very presence the British frigate was going to upset the whole campaign for the day. He swore fluently and with feeling, while his second-in-command said nothing for some time. At length, when Moreau judged his captain to be in danger of running out of breath, if not words, he asked quietly :

'Then?' The voice, cold as a drawn sword on a winter morning, brought the voluble captain up all standing, at the same time that it emphasized the dependence of one man on the other.

'We shall draw him away from the convoy. Last year we ran away from him. But our bottom was cleaner than it is now. We shall see, perhaps the same will happen again – perhaps not. If it does – well and good. We will lead him away, then turn back towards the convoy and get there first. When we have captured them, and put our brig prize-crews aboard, he will not, I fancy, attack four ships. If he does, the end will serve him right.' Epron was talking his way back to confidence.

'And if we do not sail faster than he?' Moreau asked, breaking up Epron's speculation.

'Then of course we shall have to fight him – if he wants to.' Epron mused on, 'Half as much again in weight of broadside, and double the number of men.'

'The British are so conceited that they will always fight.'

'Be fair, my friend. Be fair. He does not yet know the full extent of the odds.'

'Frigate tacking now.' The hail from the masthead reached the two men.

Moreau glanced at his captain.

'We will do nothing until we can see him from here. Were we to alter course now, we'd have great difficulty in deciding who is the faster and when to turn back for the convoy. Also we should get too far away from our prey. Now that he has turned towards us it will not be long before we see his sails from the deck.'

'If you wait until you see too much of him he'll be on top of you before we've got the stu'n'sails off her and the ship on the other tack.'

'I shan't wait that long. I'll start to take in the light sails as soon as I can see him.'

'There, sir. There.' The ensign of the watch was pointing over the starboard bow.

It was true. Moreau could see it, and Epron could see it – a tiny rectangle of white that glistened in the sunlight. It was too steadily there to be a seabird, and yet, because it was a moving thing, it held a fascination for them both.

Epron turned to Moreau and found the man's eyes already on him.

'Let's go,' he said.

CHAPTER NINE

'Both watches on deck – All hands 'bout ship – All hands on deck to tack.' The shouts of the boatswain's mates of the *San Fiorenzo* followed their hurrying figures as one went forward on either side, so that there could be no chance of skulpers not hearing the order.

The quiet of the ship was shattered by the sudden uprising on the mess deck as the eighty men of the watch below rose from their breakfast. Slamming down the metal mess kids they hastily slipped half-finished bowls into the garlands that swung above the tables. Jostling each other on the broad ladders they pounded their way to their several stations; while amongst the thickening throng on deck the petty officers moved, calling for and mustering the men of their own parties.

'Lee main brace is your station, Hopkins. Who in hell ever gave you to think you'd be trusted on the weather side. Come along, Sampson. Where the hell have you been? 'eads! You're allus in the bleeding 'eads. Stand by to raise tacks and sheets. Stand by your braces.'

The boatswain, swinging a rattan cane from one hand, hurried up and down the waist, cursing here a laggard, there a man who, anticipating the detailed order, had cast off from the belaying pin more than the regulation turns. In this ship he carried the cane only as a mark of his rating, although on many ships this form of 'starting' men to their duty was still used, in spite of the Admiralty's recent order abolishing the practice.

Dunnovan, the master, was at the barricade at the fore end of the quarterdeck. Seeing the ship ready, he turned his head towards the captain, and, receiving from him a nod, turned back to his work. 'Ready-ho-ready.' His voice raised clear gave the anticipatory order. For a second he paused, hearing it repeated on the deck below by the boatswain's mates, and on the quarterdeck by his own personal assistant, Tulloch, the master's mate.

'Helm a-lee.' The order, echoed only by the master's mate, set the two quartermasters spinning the twin wheels. The ship lifted herself from the sea. The tall masts swung nearer the perpendicular. The luff of a sail fluttered and fell back with a slap that was clearly audible. 'Helm's a-lee,' the confirmation reached the master.

'Raise tacks and sheets – leggo your bowlines.' Parties of men were working on both sides of the waist. The deep-cut lower corners of the fore and mainsails rose in the air, so that when the yards were swung their sheet blocks would clear the gunwales.

'Haul over the boom.' The order set a party of men on the weather quarterdeck hauling in the sheet of the spanker so that the wind, catching it, would help her head to come up. She was nearly into the wind. One by one the sails had lifted, flapped fiercely, and then lain still, pressed against the mast.

The crux of the manoeuvre was approaching, with the ship barely making way through the seas. Dunnovan's judgement must be exact or she would fall back on the same tack from which she had started. Hardinge would dearly have liked to make the vital decision, but, as captain, he could only give the order to tack, and the pleasure of handling the intricate sailing machine was the master's. In his own thoughts he cried 'Now – now', and heard Dunnovan's order repeated in loud tones all over the ship.

'Mainsail haul. Off all haul,' followed a moment later by, 'Back your staysails.' In a moment the men who had waited in silent groups sprang to vociferous life. The heavy yards were swinging over to the yelping cries of those that hauled the braces; in contrast to them smaller silent parties, on what would now be the weather side, had only to check away the long lengths of rope that were fed slowly into the jaws of the blocks. For one moment there was only the rhythmical chant, then for a short space a mast-shaking pandemonium existed aloft as one by one, and often more than one together, the sails flogged in the wind before they filled on the new tack – and silence settled about the tall masts. The ship had passed through the wind's eye. She was a-round!

'Right your helm. Let draw staysails.'

It was, Hardinge thought, a thrill that was always different from the one before. Watch in hand, he moved up behind the master, who had just given his final order, 'Haul taut your braces. Haul your bowlines.'

'Not bad, Mr Dunnovan. Not bad at all,' the captain commended, slipping his watch back into his waistcoat pocket. 'I made it just three minutes fifteen seconds since I gave the order to tack. Not bad when half the men were at breakfast.'

'Thank you, sir. They're a good lot considering that more'n half of 'em come from the press gang or crimps.' Dunnovan, the merchant sailor, could never quite be reconciled to the fact that impressed men could, in a few months, be turned into first-class seamen; and he utterly failed to see that the remarkable transformation was largely due to the care and attention that he and his mates had given to their tuition. Now he turned to the helmsman. 'How's her head?'

'East nor' east a half east, sir.'

The master glanced up at the luffs of the fore and main topsails, and then turned back to the captain. 'She'd probably lay a quarter of a point nearer the wind, sir.'

'I don't think that will be necessary, Mr Dunnovan,' Hardinge answered, addressing his next remark to Dawson, 'Where's the ship now?'

Going to the barricade, Dawson hailed the masthead. 'Where-away?'

'Fine on the port bow, sir,' the answer filtered down from aloft.

'He's after the convoy, all right,' the captain said. 'You can lay her a point off the wind. We'll close him as fast as we can – must keep between him and the convoy.'

'East a half north it is, sir.'

'Both watches secure. Stand fast, morning watchmen.' The boatswain's mates were piping again. Relieved, the men who had been disturbed hurried below to their interrupted meal. The boatswain's party on deck, headed by the yeoman of the sheets, were going round the ship taking short pulls at each brace to get in the last inch of slack. Snatches of song rose as the men hauled together.

The shadows of the sails that had lain across the deck had shifted, and now lay on the other diagonal. The ship's cat, who had been comfortably asleep in the shot-rack of number five gun, found itself in the shadow cast by the foresail. It rose on stiff legs, arched its back and then, flicking each hind leg alternately, started off across the deck, tail held upright like a mast.

'Napoleon, you old rake, if you'd listen out for the pipe you'd move before the sun left you. "Hands to dinner" is the only pipe you ever hears.' Simons, gun-captain of one of the after carronades, motioned the animal on its way with an affectional toe.

'Looks like it swallowed the hour-glass,' Beer answered him.

'Hour-glass? That ain't no hour-glass – that's kittens.'

'Come on, lads – down below to finish our breakfast. What are you two a-playing at. Cat's yeoman?' Lancarrow urged the others down the ladder to the deck below.

The captain watched while Dawson once more climbed to the maintopmast cap. This time he went and returned more slowly, for he had carried with him a telescope, and spent some minutes in a close scrutiny of the approaching ship.

'Well?' the captain asked as his first lieutenant returned to the quarterdeck.

'She's a Frenchman all right, sir. Frigate by the looks of her – and to be more particular – our old friend the *Piemontaise*. I can't be quite sure, for she's still all of twelve mile away. When we chased her last August she'd three or four new cloths in the bunt of the foretopsail. They're weathered a bit now, but you can still see 'em.'

'Ah, yes – thank you, Mr Dawson.' Hardinge, although in reality concerned enough, set himself to pretend unconcern. Over the edge of the sea, still invisible from the deck, was an enemy frigate. To him chance had come – the chance to carve his name on the roll of captains who have fought a successful single-ship action. It was the most difficult, most intriguing action of all : there was no senior officer to intrude with urgent signals of his own, and no grand battle strategy to interfere with tactics. Both sides were free to circle each other, seeking both a weakness in their opponent's defence and, if none appeared, then an opportunity to use their own strength to open a cleft in their rival's armour.

But for Hardinge elation was tinged with caution. The men he'd landed left him woefully short. The *Piemontaise,* if in truth it was that ship, had twelve more guns than he, and although her main deck armament was, like his, composed of eighteen-pounders, her twelve carronades threw thirty-six pound shot against his thirty-two pound balls. Chance may have come to him – and he'd accept it gladly. It was only a pity that the contestants would not be more evenly matched.

'You'll go to Divisions, sir?' Dawson's query brought his mind back to the immediate present. It would be some time before the enemy was even hull up from the deck; an hour or more before they could possibly expect to be close enough for action even should the Frenchman hold to his present course. No reason at all to upset the routine just because they were going to fight the ship an unspecified number of hours and minutes ahead. Besides, it would be bad for the men. They must accept action as part of the routine. Clean ship, ammunition ship, store ship; there was a drill and a routine for everything, and 'beat to quarters' was only another drill.

'Yes please, Mr Dawson.'

Hardinge glanced round the horizon. The convoy on the starboard beam was now some miles away, and

the enemy was on his port bow. He should, he thought,
be able to intercept any direct attack. It was well to
leave the ship on her present course until time should
clarify the position. Fate had ordained that he could
hardly have been better placed. But, if the fates had
been weaving a skein, a number of others had a hand
in the matter.

To enable his men to fulfil their destiny certain
events, completely outside the knowledge of many of
them, had to have taken place. Over a period not
of months but of years the chain that led to this meeting had been forged by many hands. A French colonial
governor sent to an uninhabited island in the middle of
the preceding century had so developed the mono-
culture of the lucrative sugar crop that the Ile de
France had never been able to provide enough food for
its growing population. A British general, making an
alliance with a native ruler had, a few years before,
driven the French from their Indian factories and cut
the supplies on which the Isle depended. Drawing
nearer in time, a British Admiral, thinking he could
achieve his object before the French would again send
their raiders to the coast, had taken himself and the bulk
of his fleet a thousand miles away to reduce a Dutch
dependency. Decaen, the successor to Governor Labor-
donnais, driven desperately for want of provisions and
learning of the temporarily undefended state of the
Indian coast, had hurried his cruisers to sea – although
by doing so he had very much reduced the time allowed
them for refit.

A merchant captain bound for Bombay to Colombo
had (probably at night or he would surely have been
captured) sighted the enemy frigate, recognized her for
what she was, and reported her presence. Governor
Maitland of Ceylon had sent a junior officer in a fast

sailing dhow to overtake and recall an almost equally fast frigate. Yet, because the *San Fiorenzo*'s speed had been reduced to that of the merchantman she convoyed, the chase had been successful. Retracing her steps half across the Bay of Bengal, the warship's crew had fought her through a gale – determination to do their duty in opposition to good seamanship. Fortune, or fortitude, had tipped the delicately balanced scale, and the British frigate had arrived in time to offer battle to the French.

Caught in the mill of great issues, Hardinge and his men – no less than Epron and his – were forced to fight; but in the particular, and whether they liked it or not, they must do so from pre-ordained footholds and against predestined odds.

The captain glanced down at his watch. 'How very fortunate, Mr Dawson, that you were able to jam the brace when the mainyard went adrift.' It was not always easy for a captain to find the right words of comment and commendation : quite impossible for Dawson to return the compliment and point out that it was only Hardinge's own determination that had brought them there in time. In any case the captain had given his officer no chance to reply but had, rather self-consciously, turned and gone below immediately he had finished the sentence, for he knew that King would have ready, at precisely ten minutes to eight, a steaming bowl of chocolate.

CHAPTER TEN

At the precise moment that Dawson, who had just called the ship's company to attention, approached the companionway that led to the captain's quarters, Hardinge's bare head appeared as he climbed on deck and unconcernedly adjusted his cocked hat.

From the break of the poop the scene was full of brilliant colour as the ship's company mustered at Sunday Morning Divisions, colour which was seen in alternate tones as the shadows of the sails lay in patterned bars across the deck: shadows that crept continually back and forth as the ship heaved herself steadily over the waves.

The black-barrelled guns in the scarlet carriages formed a continuous repetition on either side of the deck. Above them, like a notched frieze, the line of white hammicoes topped the deep and white-painted gunwale. White trousers flapped in the breeze that spilled from the great sails above. Sunburnt arms and necks protruded from the tight blue-striped jerseys. The line of black-varnished straw hats rose at each end of a division and dipped in the centre, where stood the shortest man. Before the ranks were the divisional lieutenants in blue swallow-tailed coats over white trousers, the captain of the respective 'top' and a midshipman.

From among the carpet of colours arranged on deck, the yellow masts rose upwards, black-banded by the wolds and enmeshed in the many halyards that came down to the scarlet-painted bitt-rails at their base.

Between the fore and mainmasts the boats were chocked on skids that stretched from gunwale to gunwale. Both the big launch and the smaller cutter, bluff-bowed to carry the weight of a three-pounder gun on a swivel, had black-varnished topsides above their white-painted bottoms, while their delicate sterns were picked out with yellow scrollwork. Nestling within each of the large boats were the smaller ones, the jolly boat, and the captain's particular pride – the eight-oared gig. The latter, a long slender pencil of a boat, whose black topsides shone with enamel, carried, not yellow paint, but real gold leaf upon her gingerbread-work.

Satisfied with all that he saw, the captain spoke over his shoulder. 'Stand the men at ease, Mr Dawson,' and then, when the order had been passed, 'Anything special today?'

The question took his first lieutenant by surprise. With the ship in chase of a powerful enemy it would appear that quite a lot of special events might be expected. On the other hand Dawson's passion for an ordered existence appreciated the ordinariness of the question.

'No, sir, I had thought of airing bedding and fumigating the lower deck.'

'I don't think I should do so – not today. We don't want to have to re-stow the hammicoes before we can beat to quarters. You'd better carry out the ordinary routine and then send the hands to drill at the guns. Please God we'll be making use of the practice. You'd best come to my cabin when you've told off the hands, and we'll see what we can do to make up for the men that are sick ashore. You can tell Mr Dunnovan that I want her kept sailing to the utmost. Have a party to wet down the sails. Frankly I'm never sure how much good it does, but the men believe in it, and that's what

18

matters most.' The captain paused.

'Aye aye, sir,' Dawson murmured.

'I'll be about all the forenoon. I ought to be working on these ammunition returns, but I think a chase should absolve me. Although the secretary of the Admiralty, blast his eyes, would doubtless disagree. D'ye know, he's threatened to withhold the pay of all captains who fail to render their returns within three months. Where on earth does he think we are—cruising off the Nore?'

'Has he, sir?' Dawson remarked conversationally.

'Indeed he has—the penalties of command, Number One.'

'Permission to carry on, sir?' Dawson brought the captain, who could, he knew, be almost garrulous when he was excited, to the immediate consideration of the needs of the ship.

'Yes, please, Mr Dawson.' Hardinge wondered if he had been tactless to mention the problems of command to Dawson, who had little chance of ever feeling their weight. He was sorry now that the remark had escaped him. How difficult it was, he thought, to live so close to a man who must always be aware of his own shortcomings, and for whom one had such a deep attachment. Although Hardinge could never have imagined himself in his first lieutenant's shoes, at the same time he had sufficient perspicacity to understand the older man's position. The two men were so dissimilar in character that the ambitious Hardinge, to whom the power of command came naturally, could never have understood the resigned peace of mind of his junior. As it happened, Dawson had thought nothing at all of the remark.

'Mr Dawson,' he called, just as that officer reached the head of the ladder.

'Sir?' The first lieutenant turned back.

'She looks very smart today. Does you credit.'

'Thank you, sir. Thank you.'

A pleased smile creased Dawson's weatherbeaten face. Satisfied, the captain turned and went down to his cabin.

He had beneath his feet one of the fastest frigates in the Royal Navy, and in the previous November and December she had been refitted by Bombay dockyard and her bottom scrubbed. He felt sure that he would be able to avenge himself for the time, in August of the year before, when the *Piemontaise* had shown him a clean pair of heels. Barnacles grew fast in the bright light of the tropic seas, making ships that depend on sails not only slow but, even more important in battle, unhandy and sluggish to manoeuvre. With the comparatively clean state of his own copper, he should be able to make this one advantage a decisive factor, both to catch and to destroy the more powerful enemy. Thinking it over, he was forced to the conclusion that the *Piemontaise* had not been docked, for in the months since he had seen her she had taken a number of prizes on the coast and had been back to the Ile de France – a two thousand mile trip. The comparative states of the ships' bottoms, as allied to tactics, might well outweigh his appalling disadvantages in a fight against a ship whose broadside weight of metal was greater by a third.

And he was going in to attack. No other consideration ever crossed his mind. Last time the enemy had run away; run over the horizon and left him, once her sails had sunk beyond the hard rim of the sea, with nothing to look at. This time it was going to be different. As each hour followed the one before, the enemy would be brought nearer, until both ships were in the centre of the blue circle that was the ever-shifting horizon of the sea. And when he had her there, and at point-blank range, then for one or the other ship it would be capture or death.

A knot of officers milled round the weather mizzen rigging and spread out along the rail with telescopes raised and backs bent like bows. Dawson's glass was first down and his face turned towards the captain.

'She's in sight, sir. Two points on the port bow.'

'Very well.'

'She's taking in her stu'n'sails.'

'Very well.' So the Frenchman was not going to do what he himself would have done had he been her captain. He would have gone straight for the convoy and, if he had had to fight off the escort as he did so, well and good. He must now keep between the enemy and the convoy. 'Let her fall off a point, and trim your braces accordingly.'

'Course east a half south, sir.'

Hardinge walked slowly to the weather rail, drawing out his telescope as he did so. Even with the naked eye he could see her plainly; a speck composed of still smaller specks, like a cluster of seed pearls – but through the glass these were magnified to recognizable canvas shapes. Most of them were square, hard and curved, but some were loosed and bellying as her men fought to brail up the light auxiliary sails. A flash of black showed beneath the creamy whiteness, and the captain instantly recognized it as the hull of his opponent. In the moment of mutual recognition Epron too had his glass trained on the enemy and across eight miles of water the captains' glances crossed as swordsmen stand 'on guard'.

BOOK TWO

THE FIRST DAY

CHAPTER ONE

Hardinge paused in his pacing of the quarterdeck to survey the scene and ponder on the fate which so cunningly had brought the three components of the scene together, and even set them at the corners of an equilateral triangle. The tracks that led to the meeting, recorded on thumbed and salt-stained charts, he saw as the radiating spokes of a spider's web. The convoy sailing from one port with the trade wind, had left a wake that was straight and undeviating. From another port, across a thousand miles of sea, the Frenchman had set forth some two months before: her line, a wandering tenuous affair, of long stretches in first one and then another direction as, with infinite patience, she clawed her way to windward. While from yet a third direction he himself had sailed for the protection of the merchantmen, his tracks a series of short zig-zags across the route he knew that they must take.

Raising his telescope to look with satisfaction at his opponent, he thought how often that circle of glass had held the image of a retreating Frenchman. Then, more cautiously, he reminded himself that this was not an enemy frigate, surprised in the Bay of Biscay, and which, denatured by the British blockade, was running for shelter to Brest, but a war-experienced and notorious raider with many captures to her credit. If, by turning away, her captain appeared to have discarded the spear of the hunter for the buckler of the chased, it was only a temporary exchange of parts, and one that had been made in the hope of taking both the convoy and his own interfering self.

If the Frenchman had given him credit for more strength than in fact he possessed, Hardinge was glad enough of the respite. For during the working hours of Friday and Saturday his depleted crew had been so busily engaged with the immediate need to refurbish the ship after the gale, that the almost as important matter of re-organizing the ship's gunnery had still to be dealt with.

Some six miles on his starboard beam he could see the three merchantmen. They were steering south-east and making about four knots. Slightly on the port bow, and the same distance away, the enemy frigate steered to the east. Whether he overhauled her or not, the longer the warship held this course the further they would draw from the convoy, and, provided his own speed were no less, his chance of intercepting would be greater when the captain should decide to run down for the convoy. If he had guessed correctly the Frenchman's intention, he thought that her captain must be banking on a repetition of last year's performance. Knowing the state of his own ship's bottom, he felt sure that the French had committed a grave error and by turning away had, in addition, thrown aside much of the moral advantage they might have held.

The wind, although it was unlikely in that month and latitude to die altogether, would certainly ease about midday and freshen again towards sundown. It would be some hours before either captain would know for certain which had the faster ship. It would be a matter of many hours before he could expect the issue to be joined.

'Mr Marsingal,' the captain called to the midshipman of the watch. 'My compliments to Mr Dawson, and will he be so good as to come to my cabin as soon as he has breakfasted.'

Without waiting for a reply he went to the top of the companionway, took a quick look round to see everything in order, and disappeared below.

CHAPTER TWO

Hardinge always enjoyed the entry into his home; for here, in contrast to the crowded order of the rest of the ship, he could find peace and a sense of spaciousness. The low beams, the deep window seat and small panes in the windows gave the place the tranquil air of a country house. Seen from the door almost every line was a curve. The camber of the deck was repeated in the beams above. The cunningly constructed lines of the windows bent two ways, in plan as well as elevation. At both the after corners were two half-moon shaped closets which held, behind panelled doors, the lavatory and the wash-basin.

The light, reflected from the swirling wake, passed upward through the sloping glass to throw continually rippling reflections on the pale green paint of the panelled deckhead above. The first sensation on entering was one of quiet; yet it was not the silence of loneliness but of companionship. The constant movement of light had the effect of making the cabin appear inhabited by friendly spirits, an illusion enhanced by the perpetual murmur of the wooden bulkheads which became apparent as the ship moved in the sea; while every now and then the whispering voices were overtopped by the deep rumble of the rudder as it worked on its post below the transom.

The captain stood before the desk whose top was a rectangle of leather, the edge gold-embossed where the wood had been recessed to take the covering. The gilt, he noticed, was discoloured where his cuffs had scuffed the fancy-work to a pleasant ripeness, and the nearby wood had been worn by the buttons of his coat. Even without the excitement of the chase, he would very much rather look at these things which were his own and familiar than face the pile of ammunition returns which Milne had optimistically placed there for his attention.

A vigorous knock sounded on the door. With relief Hardinge seized a sheaf of forms and flung them into a drawer. 'Come in, Dawson,' he called as he moved to the transom, 'and take some fruit from the bowl. I'll thank you to bring me an orange.' Settling himself on the window seat, he crossed his legs and leant back with his elbow through the open window. 'I do enjoy sitting at a stern window, tearing an orange to pieces with my teeth and spitting the trash into the sea – most satisfying. Queer how well the colour stands out against the blue. Come and sit down yourself.'

Dawson seated himself with deference on the edge of the transom and waited expectantly for his captain to begin.

'We'll have to exercise the great guns.'

'Yes, sir.'

'Have to do some thinking first – choose between doing our best for the armament and cutting down on sailtrimmers and the like. In fact we can't afford any sailtrimmers.' The captain spat expertly into the wake and watched the fragment float astern. 'She's sailing well. I can give you the speed to within a quarter of a knot. King is always complaining of the number of oranges I eat when I'm particularly interested in our speed.'

'King's a good steward.'

'He's going to be a good gunner, damaged leg or no. So are a lot of others – cooks, clerks, and carpenters! We haven't a man to spare.'

'You won't bother about musketry, sir?'

'No. The marines will have to help with the guns. It will mean having no one in the tops, but we can't help that. We need ten men on each long gun, four men on each carronade. That's a hundred and fifty-eight men. Now what have we got that we can't dispense with? One captain, three lieutenants, three midshipmen, one master and his mate, the surgeon, his mate and loblolly boys – another four, the boatswain and one mate – the other boatswain's mates will have to work at the guns; we must have four gunners' mates and two quartermasters. I suppose we can manage with eight men for cartridge supply? What do you make the extras?'

'Twenty-nine, sir.'

'Twenty-nine men we can't do without, and one hundred and fifty-eight at the guns makes a total of one eight nine – and we've only one seven six aboard. Thirteen men short of the very minimum!'

'The thirteen main deck guns will have to go short of a man each. We can't take any away from the carronades.'

'It's very much to be deplored, but it's the only way. You'd best dispense with the inboard men on the left and give the bag-aprons to the gun-captains. They won't like it, but it can't be helped. It will mean they'll be a little hindered in pointing the gun because there will be two men on one crowbar and only one on the other.'

'What about cartridges, sir?'

'We can't afford any men for the magazine. You'd best get enough made up this forenoon to fill all the boxes at the guns. I don't like breaking down powder out here in the tropics, but again we can't be choosers. If there's any lull in the action at all, you'll have to get a party down below filling powder bags as soon as you can.'

'Aye aye, sir.'

'I think that's all, Dawson. Get the cartridge party under way now. We'll exercise the guns at eleven, but at half past ten come for me here and we'll go down together to see how they're getting on in the magazine. If they don't look as if they'll have enough made up by then, we can put back the time of the exercise until they're ready.'

At half past ten Dawson again knocked at the door of the captain's cabin, and, when Hardinge had collected his hat, the two officers set off together. Passing along the flat, they came out through the door into the open waist and the sunshine. Then forward of the mainmast they went down the ladder on to the berth deck below, turned forward, and made their way along the narrow gangway between the inboard ends of the mess-tables and the hatches, to the hold below. At the forward end of this space, on the starboard side, was the gunner's store and underneath it the powder magazine. The filling-room was set half in the store and half in the magazine below, thus enabling the canvas bags to be drawn from the store and the barrels of powder from below. The room was lit by candles placed behind glass in little bow-windowed embrasures, for no uncovered light could be allowed in this place, which from its position was necessarily denied daylight. In most British ships, particularly those of war-time contruction, the candles were protected only by flat glass panes. But the *San Fiorenzo* had been built when superior workmanship was still considered the due of a King's ship, and in her the architraves of these oriel windows were delicately carved.

In the middle of the filling-room was a lead-lined trough that would more than accommodate the contents of a barrel of powder. Round the trough six men filled canvas bags with the black powder, checked the weight on the scales before they tied up the bags with tape and loaded them into the salt-boxes. Once a storage box was filled, it was passed through a low door that led to the passage between the gunner's store and the sailroom on the opposite side of the ship. Then it was gathered up and carried off to a gun.

Without canvas shoes the captain and first lieutenant dared go no farther, for any spark would set off an explosion that none could prevent from spreading to the magazine below.

'Well, Bird, how's she go?' Hardinge asked.

'Last box just a-coming up now, sir,' the gunner answered from his place at the trough.

The captain and Dawson made their way back to the gundeck and climbed the weather ladder to the quarterdeck.

The chase was still on the same bearing, but after nearly three hours sailing the quarry already appeared closer. The captain rubbed his hands with delight.

'We've got the legs of her, Mr Dawson,' he remarked, giving the appellation 'Mister' now that they were on the quarterdeck and might be overheard. 'You've warned the men?'

'Twas piped an hour ago, sir.'

'Then we'll go to gun drill at eleven, if you please.'

The guns were being exercised, and the guns' crews, variously stricken by sickness, evened up so that none should be weaker than another. It was an exhausting task, and took longer to accomplish than either the captain or first lieutenant had allowed. The officers of quarters had much to occupy them, and the gun-captains were in despair. Over and over the drill they went.

'Come on, you silly bastards. Now we'll go through it all again. The captain of the gun – that's me, an' don't any of you swabbers forget it, not for a bleeding moment – I faces the port 'ole. The man on the right an' left of the gun face y'r gun. I sez face the bloody gun, O'Dornell, an' that don't mean the foretopmast – this 'ere's the gun. You faces y'r gun dressed by the elbows of the man next you; you keeps y'r head up, y'r eyes fixed on me, see; y'r body upright, arms 'anging down, 'ands open and flat upon your thighs.'

The scene had all the vexation of a dress rehearsal – surprising in a frigate who thought herself smart.

Soon after noon, as expected by all, the wind had eased and now that its hand pressed more lightly on the canvas towers, it sometimes happened that a wave larger than its fellows caused the ship to roll. Then sails flapped, masts groaned and yards creaked – before the planes were once more filled by the true breeze. When this happened the quartermasters of the British frigate, feeling the deck heave beneath their feet, peered anxiously at the compass swinging in its bowl to check that no error in steering had caused the luffs of the sails to lift; the officer of the watch, after casting his eyes aloft to the maintopsails luff, scanned the sea's surface to determine by the wind-ruffles on the waves whether any man could have avoided the occurrence. Satisfied that nothing could have prevented the momentary pause, he relaxed – but only a little. It was anxious work, and a strain on all who sought so desperately to sail their ship to best advantage.

Hardinge, sorely tempted to be on deck and yet wishing to show his confidence in his officers, had resisted the vexatious fascination of watching his ship slowly overhaul the other. He could remember his own days as a watch-keeping lieutenant, and the exasperation caused by an over-anxious captain.

CHAPTER THREE

By noon it was apparent to Epron that, as a result of his turn at eight o'clock, he was now farther away from the convoy than his pursuer. The sails of the merchantmen were still in sight pipping the southern horizon, and the British frigate had narrowed the distance between the warships to something less than five miles. The French captain could see only too clearly that there was now no chance whatever of placing his ship alongside the convoy without being intercepted and, what is more, if he were to face the inevitable engagement he now knew that if his opponent wished he would have to allow him the weather gauge. The advantage that the British frigate had gained stretched like a rapier across the intervening waters.

It was annoying enough, Epron thought, to have made a decision that later proved wrong; it was aggravating to be forced to hold to it; but it was completely unbearable to be wed to a decision when those who had approved it cast doubts upon its wisdom and withheld their agreement. And this was exactly the position in which he found himself. As the morning wore on, and threatened an afternoon that would be at least tedious, his discussion with Moreau, at times almost a wrangle, continued fitfully.

'A thousand curses on this Britisher!' Moreau, draped against the taffrail, addressed his captain over his shoulder.

'I find it strange,' Epron answered, 'that you, who are always so ready to fight, should be so cast down because you are going to have the chance.'

'Bah! This is no way to fight.'

'My friend. He who makes the first hit is not necessarily the victor. Haste could lose us more than the convoy. It is obvious that to hold the Island, we must feed the garrison; and for that one prize is not sufficient — we must take the lot. It was just for that reason that His Excellency the Governor put these lascars aboard us.'

'It is all very well for Decaen to theorize. He doesn't have to put his pretty plans into action at sea. What can a general of cavalry know about sea warfare?'

'Yet you must admit that his plan is good. To take the last ship in the convoy and throw aboard a prize crew that is large enough both to sail her and man the guns while we pass on to the next is sound tactics. He has the sense to see that in these waters the convoys are always sailing with a trade wind . . .'

'Any fool knows that,' Moreau interrupted.

'And yet, before we were so short of food and when the admiral was out here with the *Marengo* and four frigates, he failed to take convoy after convoy because he always tried to range up alongside them all, and so was continually outnumbered.'

'Linois was an old fool!'

'Admitted, my friend, admitted. And so with our plan, our lascars and our bombs, we will do better.'

'Bah — the bomb! Another damn' fool contraption. You know, Captain Epron, what I think? I think we try to be too clever! If this had been last year's cruise, you — you, Captain Epron — would already have exchanged broadsides with the frigate. You'd have used bar and chain shot, and done so much damage to his sails and rigging that we'd have been amongst the convoy an hour ago.' Moreau rolled over and laid his back against the rail. His eyes, which had insolently regarded his captain, were raised to the outer end of the mainyard where a large drum holding five hundred pounds of powder was carried in a metal cradle. As he looked, it seemed that he became impressed by its potentialities, and so, when he spoke again it was with less assurance. 'But of course, if we can drop that thing on to an enemy's deck, and provided it does explode — ?'

'It will be sure to make him strike his colours,' Epron cut in. 'To me it appears an inhuman method of warfare, but, as His Excellency argues, the effect of its explosion will rather be the cause of saving life than of destroying it. The capitulation will be that much earlier.'

'Life? Captain Epron. Life demands bread – and we have little enough of that.' Moreau rolled over again and spat into the wake. For a time both men were busy with their own thoughts. It was Epron who next broke the silence.

'I could wish the Emperor were here !'

'My God! What good would that do?' Moreau flung the words over his shoulder.

'At least he'd see how he could injure the British if only he'd sent out a proper fleet. I warrant the *Piemontaise* and *Sémillante* have done more damage than any ten of Gantaume's frigates that spend their time swinging to cables in the Rade de Brest.'

'What does he care for a small island not half the size of his own Corsica?'

'Exactly. What does he care? The British Navy is a wall thrown round Europe. The Emperor runs hither and thither within the wall. He fights great battles and makes great conquests. But where is he when it is all over? Still inside the wall! Just where he was before. I tell you, Moreau, that if he spent one fraction of the effort in looking for a hole in the circumference he'd find one. How much better it would be to provision and supply our Ile de France with a proper fleet of cruisers than to capture Rome! From the Ile we cover all the trade routes to India and the East. Look what we've done with what little he's given us! Now we are not only denied the ability to help our country, but, into the bargain we must starve. Mon Dieu, I must be careful or I mount my hobby-horse!'

'And within sight of plenty! There's enough in those three ships to provision the Ile for six months.' Moreau raised himself on one arm to gaze hungrily at the convoy whose sails were still just visible on the hard horizon.

'Yes, my friend,' Epron spoke quietly, 'a great deal depends on our taking them. For unless we or the *Sémillante* have an early success, I greatly fear the Ile de France will fall. For however many dangerous reefs surround us there, and however many guns defend our harbour, they are both alike worthless if our bellies are empty.'

Epron, hoping that he had impressed Moreau with the importance of the occasion (and so by implication raised his own stature in the little world of the ship), strutted forward towards the wheel, where he joined le Paysan, the sailing master, and began to worry that officer quite needlessly with suggestions as to the set of sails that could not have been bettered. But, if he thought that he would thus escape from his executive officer's unwelcome criticism of his decision, he was mistaken. Moreau, undraping his long length from the rail, followed his commanding officer – as inescapable as the memory of a bad dream.

'It is now quite evident that we should have held our course for the convoy,' Moreau said as he closed up upon the exasperated Epron. 'Even if the Britisher had ranged alongside, a few broadsides would have winged him. And then, if he had repaired himself and followed us, he would only have saved us the journey back to finish him off.'

'Yes, but we didn't. And now the situation is very different.'

'What will you do?'

'There is plenty of time – and in six hours it will be dark.'

'I am tired of waiting.'

'You have the wrong temperament, my friend.'

Moreau took a turn back to the after rail and stood gazing at the ship astern. The wind ruffled the lank hair that fell nearly to his shoulders – hair that had been black when the *Piemontaise* had sailed from Brest five years before, but was now streaked with iron-grey. As he came back he saw that Epron's teeth were busy with his lower lip.

'You do not appear to be so happy yourself,' the first lieutenant said, coming to a halt by the wheel.

'No man can be happy when he is interrupted in an affair of this nature.'

'What will you do?' As Moreau repeated the question his eyes ranged over the frigate's deck, which was flush from where the bowsprit with its heavy rope gammoning disappeared from view below the forward rail, to the extreme after end of the quarter-deck. The dumpy thirty-six pounder carronades sat in two regular lines and were now draped with the recently washed dhoties that the lascars had set to dry in the sun. His lips curled. 'She looks like a floating laundry.'

'That is not how the British will see us when we board.'

'When – when – when?' Moreau asked.

'All in good time. I am thinking. The moon sets soon after midnight?'

'That is so.'

'South of Cape Cormorin the nights on this coast are very dark. A haze blows off the whole length of India. You think you can see, but you can't. The horizon ends below the tip of your bowsprit, even though above the masthead you can see the stars. That will be the time to turn for the convoy. We shall find them at daylight.'

'You do not think he will arrive before?'

'Obviously I cannot be certain, but I do not think so. The wind is falling light. He has reduced the distance between us by a mile. But the lighter it falls, the slower he will be to catch us.'

'On the contrary, if his copper is cleaner than ours, he may in very light weather overtake us more quickly.'

Epron raised his shoulders and spread out his hands. 'Who can tell? Who can tell?' he asked of no one in particular.

Then at length and to Epron's intense relief, Moreau disengaged himself and stumped away forward, where he set about relieving his feelings by cursing the lascars who had dared to use the ship's cannons for clothes lines.

CHAPTER FOUR

The northerly breeze had freshened towards sundown, and at half-past five in the afternoon it was plain, even to the naked eye, that the *San Fiorenzo* was still slowly but surely overhauling the chase. Amongst the officers grouped on the quarterdeck, hearts were light at the thought of action.

On cushions taken from cabins, on pillows and mattresses, they were grouped in the narrow patch of shade cast by the spanker. With shirts open at the neck, sleeves rolled, white trousered, their feet either bare or in soft leather shoes, they lolled and enjoyed the pleasant downdraught from the big fore and aft sail that rose above their heads. The wind ruffled the hair of some, while others wore the same varnished and round straw hats as the sailors; for cocked hats were only worn at divisions, ashore, or in action. The conversation was not between individuals, but by one person to the group as a whole.

'How far away is she now?'

'A little over four miles.'

'We'll be alongside her about six bells in the First.'

'What we need is a steam engine.'

'My father knows a man in Darlington . . .'

'All right, Geordie, my father knows lots of men and none of 'em live in Darlington.'

'What we want is a steam engine.'

'Fat lot of use that would be – it only goes up and down.'

'You're wrong, you know. Even if it starts going up and down, you can make it go round and round.

Think of a man winding a bucket up a well. His back goes up and down, but the handle and shaft go round and round.'

'But I don't want to think of a man winding a bucket.'

'They'll never get a steam engine to work until they've learnt to turn metal to the same narrow limits that they can wood – look at our guns.'

'What's wrong with my guns?'

'You've only got to mention the things and the Gunnery Officer wakes up – that's the first thing that's wrong with 'em.'

'It's an odd thing that the rest of the ship belongs to all of us, but the guns remain the exclusive property of the departmental head.'

'I repeat. What's wrong with my guns?'

'My dear lad, everything. But just to begin with look at the bore. It's quarter of an inch bigger than the shot. If it wasn't for the wad, the balls would roll out of the barrel.'

'The windage in the case of the carronades is only point one-two of an inch.'

'He means it's far less.'

'He's right, "Guns". It's absurd.'

'He is, and he isn't. If there wasn't any windage the gun would burst.'

'Then the gun's wrong. Half your charge escapes round the edge of the shot. When you had a pea-shooter you chose peas that were a tight fit in the bore. All I'm trying to say is that we can't yet work metal to fine enough limits.'

'Then you've got to design machines to work the metal – same way as you turn wood.'

'Good lord. Machines to make machines. I don't think I like the look of your future world.'

'Will the "owner" attack if we get alongside her at night?'

'I reckon the gallant Hardinge will attack at the very first opportunity.'

'He took the *Atalante* by night, and won himself a sword, value one hundred guineas.'

'He's made a good start for a disappointed man.'

'Good God! What's he got to be disappointed about? A post captain at twenty-four – captain of a frigate at twenty-six. I'd not be disappointed.'

'Disappointment is relative.'

'You mean the *Pitt* job. That was a dirty piece of work at the cross-roads.'

'I reckon Sir Edward Pellew let him down.'

'Bathurst was out here and on the spot when the ship was ready. Hardinge hadn't arrived – and St Vincent isn't First Lord any longer.'

'Pellew knew he could take a chance on backing Bathurst in the *Pitt* stakes.'

'The *Pitt*'s loss was our gain.'

'It's a shame.'

'What's wrong with the old *San F.* anyway?'

'My dear lad, everything's wrong.'

'The *San F.* is the best frigate in the Royal Navy.'

'So she is, youngster, so she is. It doesn't alter the fact that her topsides are full of dry rot, and her bottom's full o' worms.'

'When Chippy was putting up a shelf in the gunner's store yesterday – no, yesterday was Saturday, it must have been the day before – he hit a nail and it wouldn't go in. So he hits it a real clout, and believe me the whole lot went in, nail, hammer head and all. You know how it is? There'll be a hard skin outside and nothing but powder within. Oh, she's rotten as hell.'

'Very soon they'll build 'em of iron instead of wood.'

'You can count me out for seagoing when that happens. Just think of it. You'll freeze in the Arctic and fry in the tropics. Imagine an iron ship out here. Think of the heat of those guns at this moment. Give me wood every time.'

'You know, if we had a steam engine . . .'

'Oh, do dry up about your steam engine.'

'It's nearly time for the "owner" to come on deck for his constitootional.'

'That madman Sir Sidney Smith got him a gold medal for his services in the gunboats at Acre.'

'That was way back in ninety-eight – ten years ago.'

'Isn't this war ever going to end or was I born to spend my earthly existence serving His Britannic Majesty?'

'Anyway, he's the best captain I've served with.'

'I like the way that he and Bill Dawson get on together.'

'Well, and who wouldn't get on with Old Bill?'

'There've been some that haven't. Bill won't play with a man who's not as straight as he is himself.'

The First Dog Watch had barely changed to the Second when, a few minutes after six, Hardinge came on deck. In any other watch his appearance would have produced a sudden rise to their feet, but dog watches were a time for relaxation, when the atmosphere of the wardroom and gunroom was allowed to percolate as far as the otherwise sacred confines of the quarterdeck. Even when he seated himself on the chest where the signal flags were stowed and crossed one leg over the other, the officers he joined had only sat up or raised themselves on their elbows in deference to their captain.

'This, I think, is the most trying time of all,' Hardinge remarked. 'But there's nothing more that we can do about it – only to pray that our old *San F.* goes on overhauling the enemy.'

'I was just saying, sir, if only we had a steam engine.'

'He's been saying that, sir, at regular intervals – like a saluting gun.' Half a dozen voices addressed the captain.

'But seriously, sir. Do you think they'll ever drive a ship with one, sir?'

'Yes, I do – but it will be a long time before one is used in a warship. You'd first have to find a gun that can be elevated and depressed as quickly as the ship can roll – and without sails to steady her she'd roll all right.'

'Will we weather the *Pie*, sir?' a midshipman asked.

'I shan't try to.'

'Why, sir?'

'Because if I did, then the Frenchman would be between me and the convoy. So long as we keep to leeward he just can't get at 'em without accepting what I've got to give.' Turning his head the captain called to the officer of the watch. 'Mr Mosey. Get me a range of the enemy, please.'

The officers watched with interest while the midshipman was sent by Mosey to fetch the sextant from its box in the lower compartment of the binnacle. A minute or two later the lieutenant was taking a sextant angle of the enemy's mainmasthead, while the midshipman was thumbing over the leaves of Innman's Tables. For a second Mosey looked over his junior's shoulder, then, 'Seven thousand three hundred, sir.'

'Very well, and thank you,' the captain answered, turning back to glance round the eager group. 'We're still sailing four feet to his three. I hope all you gentlemen are prepared for action.'

CHAPTER FIVE

At nightfall only two miles separated the ships : the ability of the *San Fiorenzo* to catch the *Piemontaise* was assured, and in any case there was the moon, now almost overhead, to help. True, it would be set by one in the morning, but before that time they hoped to have brought her to action, and if not, then at least to be so close that she could not escape.

All the British officers were on deck, waiting. Some stood about with hands on the hilts of sheathed swords, while others allowed the curved weapons to trail and clink merrily over the deck planks as they paced slowly back and forth. But, whatever their rank, they had all drawn closer to their chosen mates – companionship a consolation to tautened nerves.

From forward the deep notes of the ship's bell broke the silence. Dong-dong. Dong-dong.

'Four bells – what's her range now?' the captain asked.

Dunnovan, the master, took the sextant to the weather rail. The dew of night had misted the mirrors, and he was forced to reach into his tail pocket for a handkerchief with which to wipe them.

'Two degrees five minutes.' The waiting men hearing the master's voice announce the result, looked at each other in the gloom and smiled. The angle was greater than even the most optimistic had expected.

'A masthead height of one-five-one feet.' Midshipman Lefroy could be heard studying the tables by the light of the binnacle. 'Gives a range of one thousand three hundred and eighty-five yards.'

'Less than a mile,' someone breathed.

'We've made up a lot in the last two hours. We'll be alongside her before midnight.' Hardinge had difficulty in restraining his excitement: an excitement induced not only by the imminence of conflict but by the fact that he had decided to force that which the pundits claimed to be foolhardy – a night action.

With the *San Fiorenzo* he had more confidence than many another frigate captain would have felt in similar circumstances: and this for the reason that he had had the armourer fit to each gun a small pendulum secured so that it hung below the trunnion, where it could swing back and forth as the ship rolled. From the greased bolt which held the metal rod and its weight to the gun-carriage, a white line of paint ran vertically downward. In the smoke, noise and confusion, made doubly perplexing by the dark, the gun-captains could not otherwise be relied upon to gauge the exact moment when their ship was on an even keel. But with this, and provided the enemy could be brought to point-blank range, one of the main uncertainties of night action had been removed, and Hardinge hoped that, surprised by the accuracy of his gunfire, the *Piemontaise* could be brought to submit.

'Will you beat to quarters, sir?' Dawson asked.

'I think we might. The lads are standing around the deck instead of resting and they could just as well be preparing the ship.'

A few minutes later Miles, the Marine drummer, who had been discovered sitting with his drum beside him under the break of the poop, was beating 'quarters' in the presence of the enemy for the first time. He was only just sixteen and full of pride as, standing before the mainmast, he sent the staccato notes of the alarm into the dark warmth of the night. The long roll of the drum was punctuated by the sharp double rat-rat that denoted action on the port side.

'For the love of Heaven, young Miles, 'ow much longer you goin' to go on beating quarters?' It was Sergeant John Norris's voice that stopped the drum's roll. The sergeant, naked to the waist and with his head bound in a red handkerchief, was to captain the after gun, while Corporal Twig, likewise of the Marines, had been given the carronade on the deck above his head. Tonight there would be no scarlet-coated musketeers in the tops.

As the captain had said, the sailors had been unable to rest. Ever since dark many of those whose watch it was below had lined the rail, speculating and laying bets on when the action would begin. The groups, supplied by men who drifted up from the mess deck below, were depleted by the counter current of those who, having stared for half an hour or more, wandered down again. Now with the definite order given, there was a rush to cast off the gun lashings and load and run out the guns. But there were a great many other things to be done. All the movable bulkheads under the quarterdeck had to be struck down into the hold, so too the furniture and the officers' chests that had been already packed. The big chequered canvas carpet that covered the deck of the captain's cabin, its two-foot square painted alternately black and white, was rolled up and sent below together with his desk, table and chairs.

Wallis, the cook, had to rake the fires from beneath the two brick furnaces and with his mate strike down the big copper funnel. Surgeon Ward found his way below with his cockpit crew of loblolly boys, amongst whom was numbered old Pat Dailey, the purser's steward, who had volunteered for the cockpit to release another man for the ship, as his master James Taylor, the purser, had offered his services at a gun. There were many other strange faces on the gun-deck; King was there, his defective leg forgotten, and Carrol, one of the master's mates, Carter the carpenter and Wallis the cook. Every man jack was needed – and all were only too willing.

Lancarrow, captain of the foremost gun on the main deck and therefore hidden under the fo'c'sle, was most advantageously placed for talking.

'None o' you lads been in a night action afore? No. You ain't been in the Service a dog watch.'

'Have you?' someone asked.

'Cor, an' ain't I been. I were in the *Audacious*, seventy-four – Cap'n Shuldham Peard – Cor, he were a man. He'd flog the hide off yer. Mind you, he ran a smart ship he did. We were the first to take a Frenchman at the Nile – not that I'd call that a night action proper, 'cos then the Frogs all lay at anchor. 'Twere more like a bloody great cutting-out expedition, using line o' battle ships 'stead o' launches and cutters. But I 'ad it in mind to tell you of Sir James Saumarez off Gibraltar. That were a proper muck heap if you like. Never seen the like of it afore or since. There were the Dons and Frogs – ten ships o' the line and we had but five. The Spanish admiral, he were senior to the Frog, an' he goes and gets himself into a frigate, on account of it being safer I suppose, and begs the Frog admiral to come along o' him. Well yer know, you can't fight an action that way – not wi' your admirals sitting on their arse by the ringside.

'Then we starts shootin', but not afore it were dark; an' truth to tell we doesn't do a great deal o' damage 'cept to the *Saint Anton*, and 'er, she struck to the *Superb*. Now the *Superb*, when she makes for the *Saint Anton*, she passes clean between the *Royal Carlo* an' the *San Hermongoldo*, or some such name, and they both open their fire on her. But she goes on, and leaves those two Dons a-firing fit to bust. Guns going orf in all directions. They fights an' fights, an' 'course it's too dark by then to see if one's struck to the other or not. So the silly bastards goes on shooting until just after midnight, when the *Royal Carlo* blows up. Seems it were the only way to stop her. She were flag-ship too, so that Don admiral, he must a' had a presumption. Well, we're all peeking through the gun-ports a-waiting to see what's goin' to 'appen next – when up goes t'other. Cor, it were worse nor Portsdown Fair! More than two thousand Dons a-blowing theirselves up. That's why I'm almighty glad there's only the old *San F.* here tonight. We can't be mistook for what we're not. Fine big ships they was too – a hundred an' twenty guns apiece.'

'Now then, Lancarrow, can't you keep your gun's crew from chattering?' Lieutenant Davies appeared suddenly from round the corner of the galley.

'My gun's crew, sir? They ain't said a word, sir.' Lancarrow sounded both truthful and hurt.

Davies paused, wondering if he really had heard a snicker of laughter from amongst the men. Listening, he waited and peered round the fo'c'sle, where the only light was the dim radiance that came from half a dozen candles set in lanthorns. Perhaps it had only been a groan from the foremast, or the chirrup of a sheave in a block; perhaps he had not heard the sound at all. He turned and went back the way he had come.

CHAPTER SIX

The wind grew ever steadier as the one ship ranged alongside the other. It smelt too, and eighty miles offshore the scent of sleeping India hung on the breeze – cloyingly warm, and infinitely exciting. In its passage over the sea it had gathered a haze, and was, in the moonlight, ever so slightly visible to the eye. For all its mystery, the wind had succeeded on this night in assuming something of the material fluidity of water. Coming steadily out of the north, it pressed against the sails until the tall masts were inclined, and voiced its power in the hiss of trampled waves in whose depths there bloomed and faded the livid flash of phosphorescence as they beat against the ships' flanks.

For long minutes no human voice was raised. There was nothing more to do, and a hundred and seventy-six men waited for the order to battle with five hundred. Hardinge crossed to one of the carronades and motioned the captain of the gun to one side, knelt behind the piece. Beyond the dark bulk of the gun, the indefinite horizon crossed and recrossed the view through the square gun-port as the ship rose and fell. When the ship sank into the trough there would be nothing but the grey of the sea, paler in colour near to the ship and becoming darker as it merged into the hazy sky. In a moment the horizon swung across the port, until, as she rose to the crest, there was only star-studded blackness. Then, with a clarity that was surprising, the French frigate crept into view. As she was slowly overhauled, she appeared to creep backwards towards the centre of the square. She loomed unexpectedly close, and in the moonlight unbelievably lovely.

Now, when the ship was on an even keel the enemy was filling nearly all the port, and Hardinge could see lanthorns hoving on her deck. He rose quickly and stepped back. The captain of the gun, who still had hold of the firing lanyard, took his place.

The gunner was beside the captain.

'Open independent fire,' Hardinge gave the order.

'Independent. Shoot!'

'And sink the bastards!' The voice of an excited sailor was heard in the moment's silence while the gun-captains waited for their sights to come on.

With a series of resounding crashes the guns began to fire.

'Mr Marsingal' – Hardinge caught at the shoulder of the midshipman whose duty it was to attend him in action – 'get me the name of the man who called out.'

Through the smoke, blown back from his own guns, Hardinge saw the flashes of flame ripple down the enemy's side. A second later there came the unearthly whine of her approaching shot. The men of the *San Fiorenzo* braced themselves to receive it. Hardened men winced as the strange noise grew to a climax, and then dropped in pitch as the missiles passed over. Somewhere high up a sail flogged in the wind.

Both Hardinge and Dawson reached the barricade at the same moment; their eyes searched upward into the maze of rigging. Above the noise of their own guns the whole air was full of wailing and sobbing. A block fell with a clatter, and another. As if by magic, two jagged holes appeared in the smooth belly of the maintopsail. The t'gallant above, its weather sheet cut, flapped slowly and fiercely. The head of the main stay-sail fluttered down, its stack still holding so that its luff lay along the waist.

Seeing the danger, should the firing of the guns set the canvas alight, Dawson hurled himself down the ladder; but the boatswain was there before him, dragging clear the fallen sail. The foretopsail yard was swinging drunkenly, its weather lift cut, and the fore t'gallant sheet had parted under the strain. The luff of that sail was flapping too. To the thunder and concussion of the guns there was now added the mast-shaking reverberations from aloft.

The smoke, acrid and choking, was driven back over their own ship as the guns fired to windward. Like ghosts in a moonlit mist, the men toiled at their weapons.

'Point your gun.'

'Make ready the linstock.' A moment's pause while the gun-captain waited for the pendulum to cover the white line. Then another thunderous boom, followed almost instantaneously by a crash as two tons of metal and wood hit the deck. The gun, leaping back in its recoil, had been caught by the breechings.

'Stop the vent.'

'Sponge your gun.'

'Prepare to load.'

'Load the cartridge.'

'Ram down cartridge.' Nineteen guns leaping. Nineteen crews serving them. Two and a half minutes to fire a gun. Two minutes for a carronade.

'Shot and wad your gun.'

'Ram down shot.' It was just like a practice drill, and took no more time.

'Run out your gun.' With sweating men on the heavy tackles the lumbering brute was hauled out,

'Prime your gun.'

'Point your gun.' The crowbars eased her over the marks.

'Make ready the linstock . . .'

'Fire!' And go through the drill again. Just like drill – just like drill – only this time eighteen pounds of ball, or thirty-two pounds of carronade shell, went hurtling and singing towards an enemy.

'Captain, sir. Captain, sir.' Even with the distinctive epaulette and the gold braid on the cocked hat, it had been difficult for the midshipman to find him in the smoke.

'Yes, boy. What is it?'

'It was Newton, sir.'

'What was Newton?'

Marsingal could not understand. Surely his captain could not have forgotten so soon? 'The man who sang out, sir, when you gave the order to fire.' The midshipman sounded hurt.

'Forget it, boy. Forget it.'

Captains were strange creatures, Marsingal thought. A man sweated blood to get the information they asked for – and then they told him to 'forget it'.

Dawson rejoined the captain. Together the two men looked at the masts that rose above the swirling smoke like trees seen through an autumn fog.

'All bar shot,' Dawson shouted.

'What a cowardly way to fight! It's evident he means to run away.'

In ten minutes the first engagement was over. Letting her topsails draw the Frenchman was on her way, fore-reaching on the British frigate. With her wings tattered and torn, the *San Fiorenzo* dropped rapidly astern.

The cutting of many rope halyards and shrouds was not unexpected in battle, and the boatswain and his mates were quick to set about repairs. Only in the amount of damage was there cause for remark — that, and the hindrance which night gave to the labour, and that was a calculated risk that Hardinge had taken, not thinking that his opponent would aim only at masts and yards.

As the men strove desperately to make repairs, Dawson, who had left the quarterdeck to make a hurried inspection, returned to Hardinge.

'Any hull damage?' the captain asked.

'Not a wound, sir. I don't believe the Frenchman fired a single ball. Only three slight casualties — all from stuff falling from aloft — never heard the like of it.'

'I wonder what we did to him in return.'

'It's a pity we can't see, sir.'

'We'll see well enough tomorrow. How long to repair the damage?'

'Half an hour at most. It looks a lot worse than it is.'

'Well, I suppose we can take it that he is running away. He certainly wasn't going to stay for more. You can let it be known that as soon as the last rope is mended we'll "splice the mainbrace". Better warn the purser.'

CHAPTER SEVEN

Epron, gazing with astonishment at the damage the moonlight revealed, was as perplexed as before he had been confident. The accuracy of the British fire had come as a complete surprise; and, not knowing the steps that his opponent had taken to ensure accuracy in a night action fought on the weather side, he could only blame an unkind fate.

Momentarily alone on the upper deck, the Frenchman had time to consider the situation. He had been able to see the damage that his own shot had inflicted, as first one and then another British sail had fallen into flapping futility. Now, as the moon sank lower, and his enemy became a tall shadow to one side of the moonpath, he could see her less clearly, and had no indication as to how her repairs were proceeding. He was only amazed to see how little she had fallen astern.

Moreau brought him a detailed report of the damage. The *Piemontaise* had been hulled by over twenty shots which, tearing into her, had driven the splinters like whirling knives through her crowded decks. Three guns on the main deck had been damaged; and in two cases the carriages so badly hurt that the guns would have to be remounted before they could be used again. Outside the cockpit Surgeon Andrew reported a long queue of men holding blood-soaked clouts to flesh wounds. Many of these he said were terrible jagged slashes, which in the tropical atmosphere would take days and weeks to mend, and he had laid out ten men on the main deck abaft the mainmast for the sailmaker to sew them into their shrouds.

'He did us much damage.' Epron, hearing the report, spoke soberly.

Moreau shrugged his shoulders. 'He was lucky. It is not to be supposed that he would be so fortunate another time.'

'It is very fortunate for us that he chose to fight our lee side. Had it been the other, some of our wounds would have been below the waterline.'

'And those confounded lascars – what did I tell you?'

'You told me nothing that I could not have guessed for myself,' Epron snapped; for the lascars, at first interested spectators and later just badly scared natives, had lived up to the captain's worst fears. 'Except as a boarding party to overwhelm the enemy, they are utterly useless in action.'

'They upset our own men. It's most disturbing to have them jabbering behind our backs and no idea what they are saying.' As Moreau faced his captain he kept a watchful sailor's eye on the enemy. Referring to the ship astern he said, 'She's not dropped back so much.'

'Not enough to let us turn for the convoy without him seeing us do so,' Epron agreed.

'Even when the moon has set?'

'If she can hold us now – and I fancy she has not lost anything in the last ten minutes – she will be gaining on us when her repairs are finished.'

'What then?' Moreau asked.

'I do not think he will try another night action. Remember he cannot know what damage he has done.'

'So?'

'So we will wait until dawn. Then we will make these lascars do some useful work instead of getting in our way. With their help we should be able to handle our sails more quickly than he – particularly if we wear ship. I think we could be upon him before ever he knows what we are about.'

'Then you will fight him here – before we run down to the convoy?'

'I do not say that we shall finish him off,' Epron said. 'The convoy is so important. If we can damage him seriously, then perhaps I shall be satisfied. We can come back for him later.'

'I think we should fight him to a finish and have done with it!' Moreau was emphatic.

'And you, my friend, do not have to explain to His Excellency that while fighting with a frigate you have allowed three fine merchantmen to escape. You very well know which Decaen would rather see us take into Port Louis, the empty British frigate, or three full Indiamen. She's so old as to be nearly valueless, and would only give him a few hundred more mouths to feed.'

'If you think so badly of her, why don't you turn straight for the convoy and let her do her worst?'

'Moreau, you are a fool! You have seen the damage she did us. Old she may be, but her guns are not as rotten as the hull. More damage of a like nature and we shan't be fit either to continue the cruise or capture the convoy.'

Moreau turned to go forward again, but the captain called him back.

'Do not go – I want to outline my plan.'

'I thought you had.'

'Only the first part. After we have worn ship, we will cross him on opposite tacks; a broadside, half ball, half bar shot, should do him some serious damage.' Epron spoke rapidly; for him speech was the life-blood that could restore morale. 'We shall of course pass his lee side; then, down with our helm and, crossing his stern, rake him when we're in stays. When we come round on the same tack as he, our sails will blanket his, and we shall fore-reach upon him, and, as I have said, he is sure to have suffered damage. He'll have to change his guns' crews from starboard to port, and he'll be raked as he's doing it. Oh, he'll be in a pretty mess. We can lay the ship alongside his weather side and drop the Governor's bomb on her deck. Then the lascars can board. You of course will lead the boarding party. What do you think of that?'

'Excellent, Captain, excellent – if it works.'

'But it will work. It will work!' Epron, his face turned up to the taller man, was, in his ardour, standing on the tips of his toes. 'It will work,' he repeated, almost as if the repetition itself was a touchstone to success. Then more calmly, 'If we have two crews, don't you see that we can undertake manoeuvres that we could not otherwise contemplate. Just because the Britisher does not know that, he'll never expect us to try, and the element of surprise will be all on our side. In fact his night action has proved that he's so mad keen to fight that, when we've passed him to leeward, I'll wager he'll shorten sail to wait for us, and make our plan just that much easier to carry out.'

'I wonder,' Moreau said as he turned to go forward, and then to himself, 'Anyway, tomorrow has the answer.'

BOOK THREE

THE SECOND DAY

CHAPTER ONE

At three o'clock in the morning the *San Fiorenzo* was again drawing up on the *Piemontaise*. Epron, advised of the renewed approach of his enemy, had sleep cut short, and, half expecting his opponent to take advantage of his greater speed to claw out to windward was left wondering whether the preconceived plan could be of use or whether he must rethink his tactics.

If he still did not realize the full extent of the threat that the British held above his head, it was only because it was unusual for a ship so much the weaker to chase him for so long. Before the outbreak of this war it had been considered no disgrace for a ship of inferior force to strike her flag to one that was more heavily armed, particularly if she were to make some show of resistance by exchanging a number of broadsides. Epron, the son of a small landowner, had been trained to war when it was a much more chivalrous business than it had since become. At that time men were considered the servants of royal masters, rather than combatants for their own sincerely held convictions. Prisoners of officer's rank expected an early exchange and had little cause to fear the findings of the inevitable court martial, provided they could show that they had yielded only in face of superior force and in circumstances where prolonged resistance could not have affected the result.

But with the new war conditions had changed. Frenchmen, who soon controlled the bulk of Europe, considered the British mad to continue a war that they could not hope to win; they had no real conception that in this case the nation opposed to them was fighting for the dawn of an ideal, and thus would behave differently to one which served a master who fought for his own ends.

Epron, watching the ship astern, was unable to understand the attitude of his pursuers. Because he had never before been caught by one of the British men-of-war, he knew from hearsay only that they could not be relied upon to do the obvious. To him the action was still a game of chess where he held the greater number of men. Losses would be incurred; damage would be done to both sides; it was even conceivable that if the *San Fiorenzo* should succeed in her efforts to outmanoeuvre him, she would prevent his taking the convoy. It never occurred to him that the safety of his own ship could be endangered.

Moreau, coming on deck at four o'clock, joined Epron at the after rail. A son of the people – who as a boy had run barefoot after the tumbrils through the streets of Brest crying '*à bas les aristos*' – he had more chance than his captain of realizing that there could be wars where the common people, irrespective of political faction, really wanted to fight. Moreover, he had his own special reasons for hating the enemy, for the British admiral's declaration that he was 'a fit subject for vengeance' made him an outlaw and revoked the protection given to men whose ship had struck her flag. But not for one moment did he consider such an eventuality in conflict with the *San Fiorenzo*.

☀

Although Hardinge could have worked out to windward
ready to renew the action at daybreak with the advantage of the weather gauge, he had decided to keep between the enemy and the now far distant convoy. And to
make this decision he had been called from his cot
after only an hour and half's uneasy rest.

The problems of the British were very different to
those of their opponents, for whereas the Frenchmen
were sailing their frigate as fast as skill and ingenuity
would allow, the British captain had been forced to reduce the speed of his ship to maintain the position
he favoured – a half mile on the lee quarter of the
enemy. Aware of the weakness of his own ship, he
was still in some measure acting the part of the sheep-
dog, who, barking the while, runs after the wolf and
finds contentment in knowing his sheep are saved there-
by. For should he sink his teeth and lose the battle, his
charges would also be taken.

To reduce the speed of his ship, he had first ordered
the topmast and t'gallant staysails on both main and
mizzen to be taken in; but this proving insufficient, the
San Fiorenzo still made up on the *Piemontaise*. Bearing in mind that the wind would be freshest at dawn,
Hardinge had next relieved his ship of her jib and
lowered and furled her royals. To maintain exact
station on another sailing ship was a matter of very nice
judgement.

Epron, watching the sail-drill with interest, hoped
that the British had overdone the reduction – and time
soon proved him right. The Frenchman was quick to
seize the opportunity that his rival momentarily presented to him.

'Moreau. To quarters. Beat to quarters !'

CHAPTER TWO

'Most satisfactory, Mr Dawson. Most satisfactory. I can count at least fifteen wounds in his side.'

'How many did you count for that big gash in way of the sixth port on his main deck, sir?'

'Only one for that, although I must admit it looks as if two or three shots hit between the sixth and seventh ports.'

'I reckon three at least, sir, and that both the guns on either side will be hurt.'

'Really much more satisfactory than firing at masts and yards.'

As the light grew, the captain and first lieutenant were taking the opportunity to inspect the damage their guns had done. There was silence for a moment while the two men continued their study, then, 'What the devil's that he's got at his mainyardarm?' Hardinge asked his companion.

A moment later Dawson had found the object through his own glass.

'Looks like it's a drum of some sort, sir.'

'It is a sort of barrel – but it's heavy. Look at the iron cradle it's on.'

'It'd have to be on a cradle to clear the stu'n'sail boom.'

'That implies that he keeps it up there all the time.'

'But what would he want with a barrel there, sir?'

'Well, we can assume it's there for a purpose; if it's up, presumably it comes down, if you see what I mean, and goes off with a bang. Some sort of fancy firework.'

'What a shocking thing!'

'It would be useful enough against merchantmen, if you were to range up close alongside and drop it on their deck. Why, it must hold nearly four hundred-weight of powder.'

'I wouldn't put it past a Frenchman.'

'The weaker navy always thinks of fresh horrors, and yet I don't know that it isn't better to capture men than kill them. Ask their wives the answer to that one. There's a lot of loose thinking about these days, but it's mighty difficult to get your mind clear on the subject. Mr Congreve and his rocket ships. Lord Cochrane with his sulphur gas. What's the answer, Number One? Are these new methods more humane or not? Damned if I know! But that thing on his yardarm does mean that we'll have to be careful to keep away from him. We'll not give him a chance to lay that egg on our deck – not if we can help it.'

'Captain, sir. Something's going on aboard her.'

The two glasses that had been lowered while their owners talked were again trained on the *Piemontaise*.

'Dawson, she's seething with men.'

'Lascars too, sir. Lousy with 'em. Like maggots in a dead sheep.'

'Prize crews, like as not.'

'Or boarding parties.'

'Another reason for keeping well clear. There must be nearly five hundred men aboard.'

'And we've only . . .'

'So long as we can keep within point blank range without letting her lay us aboard, it'll not matter how many she's got.'

As they watched and waited, the clew of the enemy's spanker was seen to leave the end of the boom; the brails clutched the canvas into folds that flogged slowly in the wind, and the clew tackle grew in length as the sail was drawn up to the mast and gaff.

'She's going to wear!' Hardinge exclaimed, as he snapped shut his glass and used his naked eye to give him a better estimate of the distance between the ships. It was true. He had fallen slightly behind and the enemy frigate was turning down-wind towards him. If he were to hold his course the *Piemontaise* would pass close ahead of the *San Fiorenzo* and rake her with shot, and he'd be in no position to reply. 'Mr Dawson. Wear ship. Quartermaster, put your wheel hard up and keep it there.' If the enemy were taking the offensive he must conform to her movements.

Already Dawson had set the boatswain mate to piping, 'Both watches on deck. Hands wear ship,' and then gathering as many of the watch as happened to be in the waist, he led them to heave upon the brails of the spanker.

The long jib-boom was sweeping the horizon as, eased of the after sail, the ship began to turn more quickly. The men from below were pouring up; trained men, who separated into their organized parties.

'Clew up your mainsail. Smartly, lads, smartly.' Dawson's voice was raised.

Now the clewlines, which hauled the lower corners of the sail to the centre of the yard, spilled the wind from the big mainsail and the rudder bit into the water rather than dragged through it. 'Round in the after braces.' The men on the quarter deck laid hold of the ropes that hauled the yards and waited the expected order.

'Square the after yards.'

When the after yards had been laid square across the ship, those on the main and foremast were still full of wind and helped the rudder to turn the ship away from the wind. As she turned she became upright and rolled slightly. Watching his opponent, Hardinge, having guessed the reason for the Frenchman's sudden move, saw that good sail-drill and the nimbleness of his own frigate would prevent the enemy from achieving his object. Both the ships, which two minutes before had been steering east, had turned to the south, with the *Piemontaise* a little more than a half mile on the port quarter of the *San Fiorenzo*. The Frenchman's masts, which during the turn had been seen continually shifting one against the other, were now almost in line, and turned no more. The captain guessed that his opponent paused while he thought out the next move. Hardinge desperately wanted to fight, but on ground that he himself had chosen.

'Ease the helm.' With the turn almost completed less rudder was necessary.

'Square the foreyards.' The forward yards must be trimmed to the down-wind course. He'd not make any further alteration until he saw what the Frenchman would do.

'Steer south.'

'Gather aft your sheets. Haul out the spanker.'

And what, Hardinge wondered, would the enemy do? Her captain would be chagrined that his thrust had been parried, that the intended victim was not to be so easily surprised. The Frenchman would have to think of something else. At the same time Hardinge realized that, while for all the day and night before he had held the tactical advantage, now, if the enemy were to try to cross his stern, he would at once be put on the defensive: on the other hand, if the *Piemontaise* were to return to her previous easterly course it would indicate that she was content to resume her withdrawal. The captain did not really think the latter was a likely eventuality – not now that the enemy's guns were run out. Watching the frigate closely, he saw the masts come together until they appeared as one and her bow was pointed towards him. It could be a yaw occasioned by an inattentive quartermaster. It could be – but it wasn't.

'Port your helm. Steer west. Mr Dunnovan, I'll come to the wind on the starboard tack. Mr Dawson, as soon as she's settled on course, beat to quarters.' If the enemy was going to try to cross his stern he must turn too – and be prepared for the action he was certain the French were trying to force.

'Brace the yards sharp up.' The order was piped.

As the ship came on the wind and lay over again, the cool morning breeze that had died to the merest zephyr when they were running before it came aboard once more, but this time from over the starboard rail. Instinctively the captain and first lieutenant moved to what was now the weather side of the quarterdeck, while the junior officers – for all had come on deck at the call for 'both watches' – drifted to the lee side, where they stood looking aft and wondering.

'Haul the bowlines. Set up the weather backstays.' With the fresh turn to a westerly course completed, the last details could be attended to.

Dawson glanced questioningly towards the captain. Hardinge nodded. 'Yes please,' he said.

A moment later the drum beats rolled out, their heartening tarranta-ra answered by the sound of cheering men. The long roll of the instrument stopped short and was followed by a single beat before the whole was repeated. The one stroke told that this time it was the starboard batteries that were to be manned. The cheering, only half-heartedly suppressed by the boatswain's mates, died as the men reached their stations. Funny, Hardinge thought, how the British sailor was never so happy as when going into desperate action.

Preventer lashings were cast off, the canvas aprons were taken from the vents, ports hauled up and the guns run out. The gun-captains fussed over their charges, testing the flint-locks and pushing the rimmers down the vents to pierce the canvas cartridges in the chambers so that the powder-filled tubes could be inserted. To the upper end of the tube similarly filled cardboard cartons were fixed, and when these were broken – the last motion before firing – powder would run into the pans ready to be touched off by the flint-locks when the firing lanyards were pulled.

'I'd never before seen flint-locks used on carriage guns,' Beer, the late merchant seaman, remarked to Lancarrow as they waited.

'You don't say.'

'Do'ye like 'em?'

'If they works – they works well. An' it's a damn' sight easier than playing about with a slow match – leastways as far as the gun-captain's concerned. But as you see we always have a match tub ready nearby the guns, in case your lock don't fire.'

Hardinge, vaguely aware of the bustle around him, was watching the Frenchman, who had also completed his turn. Both ships were now steering west, and the British frigate could, if her captain had wished, have left her more powerful opponent behind. It was a moment of decision : a decision which would in part be taken with the cold logic of battle tactics, and in part would depend on his own temperament. By his movements the Frenchman had declared that if the British were willing, he was prepared to try another brush. It was up to Hardinge to pick up the gauntlet that had been flung down, or to step aside in the hope of being able to bring the enemy to action when conditions were more favourable, and when he had used his speed to steal the weather gauge. This last was a factor in his deliberations; for the *Piemontaise*, who now lay out on the weather quarter of the *San Fiorenzo*, enjoyed this advantage, and if Hardinge were to shorten sail, as he would have to do if he were to wait for her to come up, then this gauge could certainly not be wrested from the enemy.

On the other hand, to pile on sail and escape from a conflict which he had spent a day in seeking was against his inclinations, and would not improve the spirit of his men. Not many of them would understand a manoeuvre that was purely an exercise in tactics, and after the anti-climax of a withdrawal they might not, next time, come to the guns with a cheer.

It was, he thought, quite a different sort of decision to anything he had ever had to make. At Acre he had been obeying the orders of Sir Sidney Smith. The capture of the *Atalante* had called for nothing comparable – a plain case of 'cutting-out' by the ship's boats of the *Scorpion*. There'd been a deal of preparation, but once the plan had been drawn up, there had been nothing to do but see to its execution. True, he had not anticipated the sudden gale that had held them wind-bound for three days in an enemy anchorage after the capture was over, but the consequent problems had entirely related to seamanship.

This was different. He wondered what the French captain was thinking. If he knew the man's thoughts, he would be able to plan his own actions. The convoy was now some forty miles south and probably, owing to the greater speed of the two frigates, a little to the west of them. The merchantmen had a hundred and forty miles to sail before they could make the safety of Colombo harbour. Assuming the enemy frigate would make two knots more than the convoy, she could still overtake and capture them before they reached safety. With the *Terpsichore* on the other side of India and the *Pitt* away north at Karachi, only his *San Fiorenzo* could prevent disaster to the three Indiamen.

In three hours, maybe less, he could, on this tack, work out to windward of the Frenchman. At present he was still between the enemy and the convoy. To get to windward would be to let the *Piemontaise* break the circle – and once through who could say what would happen. He could imagine the President of the Court : 'But, Captain Hardinge, you had the faster ship.' Yes, it was possible that he could retrieve the situation even then – and yet instinctively he disliked the idea of letting her through. He'd held the sword over her for nearly twenty-four hours, and did not relish the thought of lowering the point.

Now he was back again to the problem of morale, with nothing settled. His thoughts had come full circle. He knew very well how his officers spoke of him, 'the gallant Hardinge'. Not facetiously, but pleasantly and with a proprietary air, as if by having him for their captain, they were themselves emboldened. Sobering thought – they probably were; in that strange way in which anything anyone does in a ship reflects and reacts in some measure on every living soul aboard. He sighed deeply. When you were put up on that horse you had to teach yourself how to ride it.

His thoughts reached a climax in indecision. 'Mr Dawson.'

'Sir?'

'Have the mainsail triced up. I'll wait for her to come down to me.'

The decision made, it seemed impossible that he had ever had difficulty in reaching it, and with a settled mind he could look with renewed interest at the *Piemontaise* bearing down under a press of sail, her guns run out, the tricolour ensigns flying from the gaff-end and from both sides of the mizzen rigging.

Once again he was aware of matters in his own ship. The men at the carronade nearest to him were engaged in a lengthy argument. He moved a pace or two nearer, 'What's all this chattering, Simons?' he asked of the gun-captain.

'We was just saying that this was the right time to start an action, sir.'

With his own problem so recently settled, Hardinge was interested to learn the reason for this statement and allowed himself to be drawn into a discussion that in other circumstances he would never have contemplated.

'Why so?' he asked.

'Well, sir,' Simons answered, 'beggin' your pardon, sir, it's like this. If we starts an action now, sir, an' some silly bastard – er – poor fellow, sir, gets his block knocked orf – well, sir, you see, sir, he's victualled for the day until noon, an' his messmates can 'ave his tot to drink his 'ealth in another world. But if he gets his number after he's had his grog – why then, sir, in a manner o' speaking we've all had it, 'im as well as us – an' no one a mite better orf.'

CHAPTER THREE

Epron had indeed been surprised at the speed with which the British captain had parried the thrust, and his rapid extrication of his ship from an unenviable position had caused the Frenchman to rethink his whole plan.

'*Sacré nom!*' he exploded as, in his rapid pacing of the quarterdeck, he passed his first lieutenant. '*Sacré nom!* What will he do next?'

'He will crowd on sail and leave us,' Moreau growled.

'He'll brace up as sharp as he can and work out to windward of us,' the captain answered as he re-passed his companion.

'That is more than probable – and now that we are so near him we can see why he sails so much better than he did seven months ago. His copper is as clean as ours is foul.' Moreau had to raise his voice as Epron's broad-shouldered back moved away from him.

Epron spun round and came back. 'Decaen is a fool. We should have been careened last time in Port Louis.'

'That alters nothing. We were sent out as we are – and must make the best of it.' Moreau shrugged his shoulders.

'And now both ships are sailing away from the convoy.' Epron stopped short and faced his officer. 'It is the convoy that matters. The convoy!' his voice was raised. 'That old frigate is nothing – a bagatelle.'

'That old frigate handed us some pretty hearty

smacks last night.'

'If I go straight for the convoy now . . .' Epron mused, ignoring the last remark.

'We'll be doing what we ought to have done yesterday.'

'We thought then that we had the faster ship. I had hoped to lead him round in a big circle with him losing distance on us all the time. Anyway, you agreed with me.'

'Captain Epron, I am your first lieutenant.'

'It is not often you are so humble.' Epron began again his pacing of the deck. The interlacing fingers of the hands that were clasped behind his back betrayed his indecision.

'*A l'Empereur,*' Moreau muttered beneath his breath.

The problem was indeed one to which there was no easy solution. Epron was unable to overtake the ship which, though weaker, had shown that she could not be ignored. He could so easily be decoyed into a long and exhausting chase of the frigate; a pursuit which, on this course, would hourly take him farther away from the merchantmen, which in turn were sailing towards a sheltering port. On the other hand, if he were to turn for the convoy, the *San Fiorenzo* would undoubtedly interfere, and he had already been taught to respect both her guns and her ability to handle sail. When he next passed Moreau he did not speak but paced by with lowered head. He must, he decided, turn for the convoy, even at the cost of throwing away the present tactical advantage he had stolen from the impudent frigate, and let the British captain do what he would. He was about to frame the word that would give the order to square away the yards when Moreau's shout made him raise his eyes to the enemy.

'Captain. Captain Epron! She's tricing up her main to wait for us!'

Together the two men watched the lower corners of the *San Fiorenzo*'s mainsail as they rose steadily above the gunwale. Caught and quilted by the bunt-lines, the big sail bellied. The implication was as plain to the French officers as if they had overheard Hardinge's conversation with Dawson. Epron's dilemma had been solved in a way that he could have hardly dared to hope; with the slower ship he was being given the chance to knock out his opponent while starting with the weather gauge.

'He is a very brave man, or a very confident one,' Epron said.

'Or just a very foolish one. He throws away all that his speed could have earned him.'

'Gailteux,' Epron addressed the quartermaster, 'let her fall off a point,' and to the master, 'Monsieur le Paysan, have the sails trimmed. I am altering course to bear down on the enemy. Moreau, prepare for action port side.' Then to the back of the first lieutenant who was already hurrying to see the order executed, 'Monsieur Moreau, oblige me by passing the word for Lieutenant Schoy and Lieutenant Hende to come at once to the quarterdeck.'

Epron fell to his pacing once more, but now the shuffle of uncertainty had been replaced by the brisk step of determination. Schoy, the gunnery officer, was the first to arrive. 'Schoy,' the captain said, 'I want this Britisher dismasted. You have already loaded?'

'Yes, Captain. Even numbered guns and carronades with bar-shot, odd numbered with ball.'

'Very good. Go round the guns and see that all are elevated correctly. Tell the captains of the guns firing ball to aim between the base of the mast and the chain-plates. The guns firing bar-shot are to be at maximum elevation; they are to aim at the tops of the lower masts.' It was only natural that Epron, with a thousand miles to carry his prizes, should aim at masts and yards which could be repaired at sea rather than do serious damage to the hulls of his victims.

'Oh, Lieutenant Hende, good morning to you.' The captain turned to the young officer who wore the uniform of the Ile de France Regiment of Artillery. 'Today perhaps we shall have a chance to drop your bomb upon an enemy deck. Everything is in order? The fuse attached?'

'Yes, Captain, we are absolutely ready. I have a match tub set in the maintop, and slow matches were lit when we beat to quarters. I have two good canonniers in the top ready to run out to the yardarm – one to light the fuse and the other to release the latch. I shall, with your permission, station myself also in the top.'

'Excellent. I will sign to you like this' – the captain moved his hand up and down. 'When I lay the ship alongside him, you will see for yourself at what time it will be best to drop the bomb – but, my God! do not let it go until you are sure that it will fall on his deck. If it were, for example, to fall between the two ships just as they touch it could blow in both our sides.'

'Have no fear, Captain. The bomb will be put upon the enemy's deck.'

'Good, good. Then to your station.'

As a matter of fact Epron had no fear of any sort. He was a brave man and quite confident *se tirer*

d'affaire. The ship that he had commanded so successfully for so long would not be the one who would
suffer most from the coming encounter. His earlier
nervousness had stemmed purely from his inability to
decide on the best tactics, but now that the opposing
captain had taken the matter out of his hands, he was
only too pleased to administer the drubbing that the
Britisher's action had invited.

CHAPTER FOUR

The guns had been handspiked round until the muzzles wooded against the sides of the ports. At first they fired slowly and individually, for, though the range was short the gunlayers must wait until they could see the enemy over their sights. Those on the *San Fiorenzo*'s starboard quarter answered those on the port bow of the *Piemontaise*. But as the Frenchman drew level, more and more could be brought into action – until the ships were sailing broadside to broadside and all guns found a target. Then, to reduce her speed to that of the intended victim, the French frigate triced up her mainsail and dropped her royal yards to the caps. The smart sail drill while the guns were fully manned did not go unnoticed on the British deck.

'How in the hell did he manage that?' It was Dawson's exclamation.

'Those confounded lascars! She has men enough to sail and fight the ship twice over,' the captain answered him.

Dawson smiled grimly. 'Then every hit will do double duty.'

'There's that to it,' Hardinge agreed.

Now for a time the guns of both ships fired at point-blank range. Shot crashed against the *San Fiorenzo*'s side or went wailing overhead. Smoke, heavy and throat-catching, hid the enemy from the gun-captains until they were firing almost blind. Bar-shot whirred and cut rigging. Blocks clattered down from aloft; the sails flogged, sullen with foreboding.

For Hardinge, events had all the unreality of a nightmare, and, as in a dream the focus of his attention was continually diverted from one scene to another by the ever-shifting pall of sunlit smoke that eddied across the view. A shot entering a main deck port had struck the carriage of a gun, and now the weapon listed sideways, useless and drunken. The wicked splinters had flown, and four men were being helped towards the hatch, down which a dead man was being carried.

Hardinge, standing at the barricade, clutched the rail. It was obvious – only too obvious – that he'd caught a tartar. Below him on the main deck the guns crashed and leaped; and with a deeper note the carronades on the fo'c'sle and quarterdeck barked and then moved back on their rollers. It wasn't going well. Clear above the smoke, and appearing unconcerned with the racket below them, the captain could make out the t'gallant masts of the enemy, bright in the sunshine. They appeared closer than they had before. Watching them, he thought that his enemy was turning towards him, bearing down upon him. Yes, she was closing, bringing with her all those men, and the queer contraption at her yardarm.

In the lee berth he was open, should his sailing machine be badly damaged, to be either crossed and raked or boarded. Hardinge was forced into a withdrawal.

'Boatswain! Pipe, sailtrimmers. Double up the guns.'

By turning slowly away from the wind and the enemy, he was on the inside circle, while the Frenchman on the outside had further to go. Even so he must be careful, for too sudden a turn would enable the enemy to cut across his stern and rake him.

'Quartermaster. Starboard your helm. Steer south-west.'

Alternatively the enemy might overlook the alteration until she had so fore-reached upon him that she would have even farther to go. Sail damage received on a down-wind course, where one sail could often blanket another, would have less relative effect on his speed than if he had kept his ship beam-on to the wind.

'Mr Dunnovan. Square away the yards.'

Either way, while the sailtrimmers were away from the guns, he would gain a little respite, for now that they were 'doubled up' one crew was serving two guns, leaving the gun-captain of one to fire his piece while the men reloaded the other. The alteration was having the desired effect. The captain could see that a great deal of the Frenchman's shot was passing ahead.

The *Piemontaise* was turning, following him round. His own ship, firing low, aiming mainly for line and not caring whether she hit with a ricochet or direct, had made little visible effect on the enemy's rigging; what had been done to her hull the smoke made impossible to see. But the change of direction allowed Hardinge at least an occasional glimpse of the enemy deck, for now that the wind was on the quarter it shifted the battle smoke forward over the lee bow. Attended by Marsingal, the captain moved as far aft as he could.

By the time the men were back at the guns both ships had altered course, and the *Piemontaise*, who had dropped back on the quarter of the British frigate, was, thanks to her undamaged sails, once more creeping level again. When she had done so, Hardinge was for the second time forced to make a forty-five degree turn to port, until the *San Fiorenzo* was running

DIAGRAM TO EXPLAIN MONDAY'S ACTION

WIND

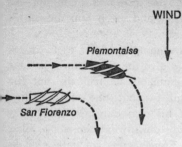

Plemontaise

San Fiorenzo

1.

Hardinge has allowed the distance to open and Epron has seized the chance and turns to starboard in an attempt to cross his enemy's bows. The *San Fiorenzo* must turn very quickly if she is to avoid receiving an attack to which her broadside guns cannot reply.

2.

Epron, tries to cross his enemy's stern. Again Hardinge must conform.

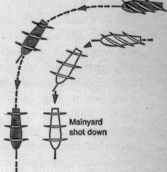

Mainyard shot down

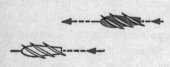

3.

Both ships have now reversed their course and Hardinge reduces sail to wait for the Frenchman to come down to him.

To Convoy **4.**

Epron bears down on Hardinge and begins a broadside engagement with intent to board. Hardinge seeing this draws off by two 45° turns.

dead before the wind. This turn had again put the Frenchman on the quarter and given him the job of working abeam once more.

The *Piemontaise* was coming in closer each time — but not yet so close as to give the appearance that she proposed to board. Presumably he had the hot fire of his own guns to thank for that. She was travelling fast — much faster than his own damaged ship. Now that the course was truly down-wind the smoke blew away forward and the French crew could be seen as black in the rigging as crows on a winter tree. They brandished knives, and there were soldiers in her tops who levelled their muskets at the unprotected British decks.

The guns roared as the sweating *San Fiorenzo*'s redoubled their efforts. The ship shuddered under the hammer blows of their repeated discharge. Hardinge had forgotten all about danger. He was entirely identified with the fighting of his ship. Davies, Moysey and Ashmore, the lieutenants of quarters, were encouraging their men. Their drawn swords glittered in the sun. The sailors shouted defiance as they worked. The discipline of common peril held the crew in new-forged bonds. The Frenchman was so close that the effect of each discharge could be seen in her shattered hull — and a moment later the gun's crew cheered hoarsely as yet another scar appeared on the enemy side.

Then, appearing momentarily on the consciousness of the men below before it crashed amongst them, something enormous fell from aloft — a ton and a half of timber, round and smooth. It crushed two men in screaming agony against the gun carriage it overset. A second later it was followed by its fellow. The mainyard had been shot through in the jeers. In two halves the largest, heaviest spar in the ship had fallen across either side of the gun deck.

The maintopsail was flogging uselessly with the clews ripped out. The *San Fiorenzo*'s speed dropped; and the *Piemontaise*, her royal yards climbing up the masts once more, swept, with her men cheering, towards the south – and the unprotected convoy.

CHAPTER FIVE

As Moreau, with the usual taciturn expression on his face, approached Epron, he saw that his captain was beside himself with delight.

'Ah, my friend, why do you look so gloomy? Did our *Piemontaise* not fight well? Cheer up, man. We have defeated him – and now for the convoy. Monsieur le Paysan, Monsieur le Paysan,' he raised his voice, 'lay me a course to intercept the convoy – but first have the stu'n'sails rigged on the main and foremast yards.' Then turning again to his first lieutenant, 'Well, what damage did our opponent do? Hey, Moreau, it was almost as good as the *Warren Hastings* over again.'

Moreau was not so easily to be raised from his melancholy. 'Captain, the British have made a sorry mess of our port side. Over fifty shot between the gunwale and the waterline. I've had the well sounded – nearly a metre in the bilges already. The master carpenters with their mates and crews are already plugging the holes. The surgeon reports another fourteen dead and thirty-six wounded . . .'

'All the more reason to get to the convoy quickly!'

'If we get them it will mean going with them to Port Louis. There's enough damage for a refit, and God alone knows what will happen if we strike bad weather.'

'Then we must take the merchantmen, and go back now while the weather is good.'

Moreau shrugged his shoulders. 'I agree. I only

hope it can be accomplished without any more interference from that . . .' He nodded to where, a good
mile astern, the *San Fiorenzo* wallowed in their wake.

'Why must you be such a pessimist, my friend?'

'I am a realist. Come below and see for yourself
what he has done to us. His guns were aimed so low
that half his shot hit after the first graze – and caused
all the more splinters for that. Richochet wounds
are the devil to plug!' Moreau paused at the ladder-
head to allow his captain precedence. 'You know we
have already used half our powder and all our bar and
chain shot. We've only ball and grape left.'

'Really, I don't think we need bother about the
San Fiorenzo any more,' Epron replied, standing on
the top step and casting a glance in the direction of
the tattered British ship. 'As you see his rigging is
badly cut up and he certainly won't have a spare
mainyard in his spar-rack. He's a dead carp as far as
we're concerned – quite dead. We'll take the convoy
by midday tomorrow, and then with the three prizes
make for Port Louis. A short cruise, my friend, but a
most successful one.'

Moreau, as he followed Epron down the ladder,
still refused to be comforted. 'I hope you're right –
but isn't there some saying about not selling the skin
until you have shot the bear?'

CHAPTER SIX

A mile behind the *Piemontaise* and slowly but surely
dropping farther and farther astern, the crew of the
San Fiorenzo were busy counting the cost of the
encounter – no one more so than her captain.

The pill that Hardinge found himself forced to
swallow was bitter indeed; and he now saw that, had
the Frenchman not been entirely pre-occupied with
the convoy he would probably be well on the way
to a French prison. He knew, now that it was too
late, that his action could only have been justified
close to the merchantmen, and then only if no other
means of saving them could be found. He should
have made use of his superior speed to gain the
advantage of the weather berth. Valour alone could
not be relied upon to defeat good tactics. Even now,
as he watched the *Piemontaise* sail off in chase of the
merchantmen, he realized that, had this been the
morning of the day before, when they were only six
miles away, nothing that he could do would save them
from annihilation.

But it could be that the Frenchman had been both
over-greedy and lacking in decision. There was more
than a chance that his crew would fish the mainyard
and re-sling it. His own ship's hull had not been
struck below the wales; she was making no more water
than usual, and all the damage was to her mast, spars
and upper deck. The Monday's tactics of the *Piemontaise*
had been applied a day too late. Her captain's greed and
the excellent work of his own men had given him a
reprieve.

Searching the recent history of the Navy he knew many cases where failure against a more powerful ship had caught the imagination of the British public and saved the captain from disgrace. But even if these unsatisfactory actions had helped to build tradition, he also knew the verdict of brother officers. 'He was lucky to get away with it' were words that could never be a passport to a further rise in his profession. There would be some who would say that he had done the best he could; that no more was expected of him; and that now the convoy must take its chance. But a man had to live with himself, and it was no answer to put a copy-book plea which in his heart he knew to be false. Before the table of a court martial his conduct could probably be defended – almost certainly so before officers who had not actually seen and experienced the circumstances. But before the bar of his own judgement he stood condemned. A momentary weakness, to which an older, more experienced captain would not have pandered, had dictated his decision to fight from a bad position. Now he could only rely on the further exertions of his officers and men to rectify the error he alone had made. Somehow or other he had to get the old *San F.* sailing again. He had to catch that damned Frenchman and give him the drubbing he deserved – and he would.

Dawson came to him with the list of casualties. Eight were dead, and fourteen wounded. Twenty-two men in all. He was now not seventy-seven but ninety-nine men short out of a ship's company of two hundred and fifty-three. Each gun would be three men short : a reduction so great that henceforward he could hardly hope for efficiency, let alone effectiveness.

Handing the list back to his first lieutenant, Hardinge

had to take firm control of himself. For the first time since he had been given command of a ship he was savouring the taste of near defeat, and did not relish it at all. The boatswain's parties were already busy getting up rope to repair the rigging, but there were still many men standing about the guns. Their eyes were turned aft towards him as they waited for the definite command which would remove their apprehension. He saw the look of patient inquiry in Dawson's eyes. The life of the ship paused while the captain made up his mind.

'Mr Dawson — have the mainyard cleared away and fished.'

'Fish the mainyard, sir?' Was his captain really going to attempt to mend the largest spar in the ship?

'Yes, Mr Dawson. The *Ajax* did it — and so can we.'

'Very good, sir. What shall we use to fish it with?'

'The stocks of the bower anchors. If we're to catch the Frenchman, we've got to have the full mainsail. It's no use trying to make do with the spare topsail yard. I'll want the main stu'n'sails set as soon as you've re-slung the yard, and we can't fit their furniture to the smaller spar.'

The realization that the battle was not to go by default, and that a great effort to overtake the enemy was to be made, was the best tonic that could have been administered to the crew who were still dazed by the beating they had taken. The guns on the port side of the main deck were turned fore and aft and hand-spiked against the ship's side to clear a space between the fore and mainmast, where the fifty foot long spar could be set up on trestles ready for the carpenters. Snatches of song could be heard as the men were set to work and laughter rose once more from groups that had been silent, and neither the boatswain nor his mates seemed to hear the chatter which in other circumstances they would at once have repressed. Discipline was changing from a convention ingrained by the Service to the perfect state where men worked and fought for the ship alone.

Hardinge watched the work from the barricade, and at the same time kept an eye on the enemy. He had to accept the fact that if the Frenchman should guess what he was doing and that the bulk of the port side main deck guns were temporarily withdrawn from the ports, the *Piemontaise* might return and cause his complete defeat, for she had only to make a circle to the eastward and engage his port battery to ensure a successful outcome. But the British captain did not think she would do so. He was already learning the character and intention of his opponent. The Frenchmen would fight fiercely and well if directly engaged, but they were more intent on securing the merchantmen than on entering into a battle *à outrance* with the escort. The *Piemontaise* was carrying out correctly the duties of a commerce raider; to evade action with enemy warships and to conserve her strength for use against her real targets.

Dunnovan had already run out the stu'n'sails on both sides of the foremast yards. But, if the following wind made the tactical position less desperate than it might otherwise have been, it made the heat almost intolerable. The sun, nearly overhead, beat down relentlessly on the men who worked on the deep-waisted gun-deck. Hardinge wondered how much longer they could stand it.

As he watched, two large groups struggled, with the aid of tackles rigged to the fore and main tops, to lift the two broken halves of the mainyard into place for repair. Other smaller parties were busy splicing the cut rigging, while larger gangs sent down the badly torn maintopsail and swayed up the spare sail from the sailroom at the forward end of the lower deck. The sail's bulk was so great that both the ladder and gratings had to be lifted clear of the main hatch before it could be brought up. In a remarkably short space of time the *San Fiorenzo*'s deck and yards had assumed the appearance of a disturbed anthill, where bodies of furiously working insects struggle with apparent confusion to re-establish absolute order.

Before moving the broken yard the sail, fortunately undamaged, had had to be cut away, and now the two halves of the naked spar were being offered up to each other so that the splintered ends interlocked. Next, tackles were secured to each half, and the yard hauled together as closely as human power could force it. Then, while the wooden anchor stocks were being taken from the anchors, and the iron bands knocked off them, the carpenters set to work with mallet and chisel to cut two deep grooves, one in the upper and the other in the lower side of the yard, into which the two eight-inch thick stocks would be fitted to bridge the join. The stocks, square-sectioned at the outer end of their twelve-foot length, were a foot deep in the centre, and to gain strength the deeper section was sunk into the yard at the join, so that when fitted into the grooves the stocks protruded a level four inches above the work. Four bolts were then passed – two on each side of the break – right through yard and stocks. To make an even surface on which to pass the wolding and to add strength to the splice, the spare capstan bars, four inches square, were next placed round the break. The whole was then bound together with three-inch rope, each turn of the wolding hauled taut by leading it through snatch blocks to the capstan. To prevent loss of tension while the rope was peeled off the drum and before the next turn could be taken round the yard, those turns that were already bound round the spar were held in place by ten-inch nails.

It had been half-past seven when the action began and five minutes past eight when the yard was shot down. By eleven o'clock Dawson, made enthusiastic by success, reported the mainyard ready for hoisting, and an hour later it was once more in its place, with the mainsail bent on. Only a few minutes then sufficed to break out and sheet home the big sail, and in a very short time the stu'n'sails on either side of the mainmast were likewise set and drawing.

With his ship repaired by the efforts of her men, Hardinge had as good a sailing machine as ever. Each time that he had spared a glance for the *Piemontaise* she had appeared smaller than before. Peering ahead he now saw that she was almost on the southeastern horizon, and the best part of twelve miles away. Twelve miles in the light March breezes of the Indian Ocean would take many hours to regain.

The hands could be sent to their dinner—and an extra tot of grog. There would be plenty of time in the afternoon to deal with the damaged gun, and for the sailmaker to sew up the dead.

CHAPTER SEVEN

In the early afternoon Hardinge was again on deck to see how the gunner and his crew were progressing in the efforts to fit a new carriage to the damaged gun.

The barrel, its flintlock unshipped, had already been laid upside down below the boats with the vent and pan resting against the deck planks. A spare gun carriage, without its wheels, had been slung by the axles from the spars on which the boats rested and, as the captain arrived, it was being lowered upon the upturned gun. The upside-down way of going to work was normal practice with the ship at sea. It was thus possible to hold the carriage, which weighed only a few hundredweights, against the swing imparted by the ship while the bolts holding the trunnion strap were driven and secured. It would have been quite impracticable to prevent the two-ton weight of the barrel from shifting.

Bird, the gunner, aware of a newcomer's presence, glanced up and touched his forelock.

'You've got along well,' the captain said.

'Us'll have 'er right-road-up afore the glass is turned again, sir.'

'It's quite cool here under the shade of the boats,' Hardinge remarked.

'Depends what yer a-doin', sir. 'Tis hot enough working.'

The captain watched until it was time for the bolts to be driven, then he tactfully moved away, for there was almost sure to be an argument between Carter the carpenter and McCulloch the Scots armourer as to who was to drive the bolts, and he had no wish to be referred to as adjudicator in such a very delicate matter. The carpenter would claim that, as they were being driven into the wood of the carriage, the work should be his; while the armourer, who had made them, would naturally conclude that as the workmanship on the gun was his responsibility, the job should be done by him.

Watching from a distance, Hardinge saw that he need have had no fear. The inevitable discussion had apparently taken place and an amicable arrangement been reached. Carter drilled the holes, while McCulloch inserted and secured the bolts.

Gratified by this evidence of co-operation, the captain went back to the quarterdeck. As he climbed the ladder his upward glance followed the slim beauty of a bosun bird that sped athwart their course, its white tern-like body with the long spike of its tail silhouetted against the blue of the sky. He paused rather breathlessly, and then continued the short climb to the deck above.

Moysey was 'keeping the deck' for the afternoon watch. In shirt sleeves and trousers the officer endeavoured to remain within the ever-shifting shadow cast by the spanker, and had chosen a position by the topsail halyard rack on the starboard side. Midshipman Lefroy was with him and the two were deep in conversation when the captain's head appeared above the deck. Expecting him to join them in the shade, the two officers half turned and paused in their conversation, but Hardinge remained in the patch of sun at the head of the ladder.

Peering forward, the captain could see the *Pie-*

montaise just on the port bow. There was no question
that she was nearer than she had been two hours before, but it would be a devil of a long time before
they could catch her again. He found it necessary
to shield his eyes to see her properly, and was aware
of an ill-defined pain behind them. A conscious effort
had to be made when his eyes shifted their focus
from the ship that was on the horizon to inspect his
own.

The *San Fiorenzo* was sailing well, with that pur-
poseful quietness felt only when all the sails were full
and drawing. Dark blue ruffles appeared on the sea
where the wind was spilled from the bellying canvas
as she rolled to leeward. The bow-wave was speaking
again and from somewhere forward a man sang as he
worked.

But Hardinge was not to be easily satisfied. He was
essentially a man of action, and found the long wait
intolerable. He wanted desperately to know if he
would be successful both in catching the enemy and
in defeating her when caught. He hoped to be successful in the first, but the second was by no means a
foregone conclusion. In fact cold reason suggested
an outcome very different from the one he hoped
for, and the one that his men were striving so hard to
obtain. If he wasn't so terribly short of men! If only
those he had were in better health. He ran his finger
round his cravat. He had felt cold for the last hour
and not a little shivery. He hoped it was only fatigue
and excitement. The damnable climate made a man ill.
The miasma came each evening from the mangrove
swamps. He was sure it was the swamps that were the
cause – those endless low-lying bogs where the im-
mature forest spread dankly from roots that were half
in the water and half in the greasy grey mud; where

little climbing fish ran like varnished mice along the
limbs of trees, and fell like nuts when the boughs were
shaken. To know where it came from one had only to
see the grey, sweat-scented mists that rose each night
from the decaying vegetation of the lagoons that lay
between the hills and the sea.

Men were healthy while the ship stayed at sea,
but once she had lain for a week or more in one of
the confounded anchorages they would be down with it.
And it would go on striking them. Just when he hoped
they were going to get free they would be down again,
with headaches, giddiness and a hell of a fever. But
perhaps it was only the sun that was making him feel
as he did.

He moved to stand in the shade of the mizzen
topsail. There the wind spilled from the arched sail
in a cool down-draught on to a deck that in other
places was heated until the pitch ran and bubbled in
the seams. After the strength of the sun, which seemed
to have sapped his own vitality, the new position
was very pleasant, and for a moment his spirits rose.
Then a cold shiver ran over his body. Starting at the
base of his spine it crept up to his shoulders and down
to his knees. His shirt, he discovered, was soaked
with perspiration. As he went down to his cabin to
change a sensation of nausea overcame him, and it
seemed that the ship rolled more heavily.

So much movement was quite surprising in such
good weather; but, as soon as he was down in the
shelter and away from the sun and wind, he felt
better. Before he turned aft towards the bulkhead
that separated his own quarters from the rest of the
ship he paused a moment to glance at the unfamiliar
aspect of the deck. Gone were the white-painted
partitions that normally made the space an alleyway

dominated by the squat and scarlet-painted bulk of the big capstan, its bars stowed in metal hooks fixed to the deck beams above. The walls of the officers' cabins and wardroom had been cleared away to expose guns, which now stood in a line that was a continuation of those in the waist that had no sheltering deck above them.

The captain opened the door to his own cabin (where the two after guns now faced the ports and took up most of the deckroom). As he did so the marine sentry, set to guard the entrance to his quarters and the ship's keyboard, came to attention smartly enough although there was that in his movements that caught the captain's attention.

Holding on to the door-post to steady himself, he looked hard and long at the marine. His own eyes, that hurt again when acutely focused, noted the tell-tale sweat that stood out on the man's forehead.

'You're sick, boy,' the captain said. Then, because he could not remain supporting himself while the man stood to attention he must, whatever the effort, release his hold of the door. The eyes of the young marine never left his captain's face.

'Begging your pardon, sir, you're not looking so well yourself.'

It was the sort of remark that only adversity could have made possible between those two men, who fought a common enemy that struck regardless of rank or position.

'Eh?' Hardinge said, surprised that his illness had been noticed, and by the man's temerity in drawing attention to it. 'Eh? Perhaps you're right. Makes you feel terrible, doesn't it?'

Without waiting for an answer he pushed on into his cabin calling for his steward. It would never do if he, the captain, were to go sick at this hour.

'King,' he called his servant, 'King, my compliments to the surgeon, and ask him to let me have a dose of bark at once. No – make it two doses, and give one to Marine Catchpole. He won't like the taste of the filthy stuff any more than I do, but it will do him good.'

Hardinge lay in his cot which, carried by a metal rod at each corner, swung from the deck-head of his sleeping-cabin. The cot, with its eighteen-inch deep canvas sides, occupied most of the clear space, for against the ship's side was number twelve gun, and on the other inboard bulkhead a shallow cupboard. There were hooks on the inside of the door that led to the great cabin, and on one of these he had hung his blue tail-coat. Now as he lay, he idly watched the garment that, in unison with the ship, moved stiffly on its hook.

The surgeon had come and gone, leaving him alone with his misery; he had arranged for Catchpole to be relieved; and King, fussing like a hen over a wet chicken, had been driven sternly away. The foul malady struck so quickly. At one moment a man would be as hale and hearty as usual, the next he would be only a pathetic shell of his normal self. Fortunately the cinchona bark acted almost as quickly as the disease, and if taken early enough in the first onset could greatly reduce the effect both of that and the subsequent attacks. Everyone on the coast knew the habits of 'country fever'; how after striking it would as suddenly relent, only to return again either the following day, the day after that, or in some cases three days later. Even the individual attacks were known to be divisible into recognized zones, and the sufferer could chart his position as the illness swept over him. He recalled the cold ague that, when he had been on the upper deck, had spread from the small of his back until it had had his whole body in its icy grip. Now hot flushes seemed to burst continuously within his belly, gradually increasing the area over which they swept until his frame was entirely lapped by their evil flame. There would follow, he knew, a time when the sweat would pour from him; then, when perspiration had released the intolerable dry heat, he would sleep, and with luck after an hour or two he would wake refreshed.

He could even hope to use the nature of the first attack to guess the day when the next would arrive. The long period of the shivers, if followed by a short period of fever, suggested the return of the disease in three days. If it were not to re-claim him for seventy-two hours, it would make little difference to the final outcome of the chase, for, win or lose, the battle must surely have been fought by then.

The anxiety of the gale, his foolhardiness of the morning, the timely meeting with the convoy, the unsatisfactory night action : the beam of his thought, made wavering by sickness, wandered back through time. A ray of light in the dusk of memory, it picked up scenes for momentary illumination and then passed on its haphazard way.

Success. He needed success. The fates could not be so cruel – not after the prolonged persistence he'd shown. Victory in this fight could again set his feet firmly on the steps of the ladder from which they'd been in danger of slipping. Success, and he'd never have to fear the caprice of an admiral again. Beyond his vision of the Frenchman as he had last seen her there was a greater ship – the ship of the line he'd

surely be given. There hadn't been much doing at
sea lately. The Emperor had crushed Prussia and
forced Russia to sign at Tilsit. No British force held
a foothold on the continent of Europe. The adminis-
tration at home would snatch eagerly at any victory.
His friend Percival, the ambitious and cunning chan-
cellor, could help him there. And beyond the great
ship of his imagination floated the accolade of knight-
hood, for it was quite usual to bestow a baronetcy on
frigate captains who defeated larger ships. Captain
Sir George? Captain Sir George could indeed hope
to become Admiral Sir George. The *Piemontaise* must
be taken!

The confounded frigate had to be brought to action.
She had to be! With a gesture of frustration he flung
himself over within the narrow confines of his cot.
His head throbbed behind his eyes. He moved restlessly murmuring with senseless repetition, as he turned
this way and that, the words of an old proverb:

> *For lack of a lynch-pin, a wheel was lost.*
> *For lack of a wheel, a gun was lost.*
> *For lack of a gun, a battle was lost.*
> *For lack of a battle, a Kingdom was lost.*

Over and over again the words repeated themselves
in his fevered brain until they ceased to have a meaning
and became only a talisman that held his mind to
some semblance of sanity.

An hour later sweat soaked his shirt and lacquered
his skin – a release from the terrible dry burning.
But his mind still savoured the words, and somehow
in his fever the last line had changed.

> *For lack of a frigate, an island was lost.*

CHAPTER EIGHT

Neither the French captain nor his second-in-command had, after the second action, expected to receive any further interference and had contentedly watched their opponent fall astern, sure that their mission would be accomplished before another twenty-four hours had passed. The sight of the *San Fiorenzo* bearing down upon them throughout the long afternoon was a sad blow to their hopes.

For a time the sextant angles taken by the master had been too small for differences to be noticeable, and there was much argument amongst the French officers gathered on the quarterdeck.

'She is nearer!'

'I don't believe it!'

'I'm sure of it! The angle may be the same – but my eyes tell me she comes nearer all the time.'

Then, when the unwelcome fact had been confirmed by le Paysan with his instrument, there was still much speculation as to how the Britisher had managed it.

Epron, with left knee bent and right extended, crouched over the after-rail. His elbows were supported on the capping to hold steady the telescope. His left eye shut twisted his face to a grimace.

'*C'est vrai. Mais c'est tout à fait incroyable!*' The captain straightened his back and turned to face the eyes of the officers around him. 'With my own eyes I saw his mainyard shot through. It is not possible that he should have a spare.' The faces showed their individual perplexity. For so long every action had run to pattern that the unusual was now doubly disconcerting.

'Then he must have fished it.' Moreau shrugged his shoulders and spoke off-handedly, as if by so doing he deliberately withdrew his sympathy from his captain.

'That is obvious,' Epron snapped. 'We can all see that he has it slung now – and his stu'n'sails are set on both sides of the main.'

'So far we have accomplished nothing at all!' Moreau's casual tone was a goad applied to flesh made raw by the futility of their endeavour.

'Twice I have forced him to withdraw from action.' Epron took a few short steps forward and then turned to face the men whose heads and shoulders had followed his movement. 'Twice he has been defeated!'

'It is only unfortunate,' Moreau answered, 'that he is so foolish that he does not understand.'

'*Sacré nom. Sacré nom de Dieu. Sacré nom!*' Epron exploded. 'He is a devil. Next time I shall certainly finish him off.'

'It would have been better had we done so this morning.' Moreau, a man of limited intelligence, found it easy to overlook that facts had altered since the morning's decision had been made.

'At the time you were glad enough to be free of his shot.' The captain did not trouble to hide the relish which he was able to bring to the statement.

'Let us return and finish him off.'

'Agreed that he badly needs a third lesson, and nothing would please me better,' Epron mused, 'but – and this is the big question – have we the time? Le Paysan,' he turned to the master.

'Captain?'

'Assuming the wind to hold, when will the merchantmen make Colombo?'

Receiving the question, le Paysan detached himself from the group and disappeared down the companion-way to his cabin where, with pencil and ruler, he busied himself over the chart.

While waiting for the answer Epron still looked over the stern with his eyes fixed on the distant enemy. It was not the usual stance for one in charge of a man-of-war, where normally he faced the way his ship was going. The many hours that he had spent looking over the wake could not inure the captain to the unusual, and yet, except for conversation, he found himself unable to take his eyes from the ship astern. 'And the prob-lem is not of time alone,' he mused on. 'For, while we are in enemy waters, damage that can't be repaired at sea is more serious for us than for the Britisher who has a welcoming port within a day's sail to leeward. Our mission is to appear and disappear from the trade routes. To snap a prize and leave before we are caught –'

'Oh! Cut the cackle and go back now!' Moreau, as if to emphasize his own impatience, turned his back on his captain.

The arrogant tone of his first lieutenant's voice suggested to Epron that to have delegated any of his authority was to have hinted at the transference of much more than he had intended. Decisions were hard enough to make, the captain thought, without his first lieutenant adding to the weight he had to carry.

Le Paysan, returning, distracted Epron's thoughts from their groove.

'You see, Moreau.' Now that the first lieutenant had turned away, Epron found himself forced to raise his voice. 'Le Paysan says that we must complete the business by tomorrow's sunset.'

'And I,' the first lieutenant flung over his shoulder, 'that we should finish off the accursed frigate here and now.'

'And I, who am the captain,' Epron shouted with some heat, 'say that we have not the time, and that it would be foolhardy to do so!'

Explosions between captain and first lieutenant were not unusual, and normally called for sympathetic rather than serious comment. But on this occasion the officers gathered on the quarterdeck felt that disagreement ran deeper than before. Seeing the force of both arguments, they did not know with which to side, and so remained silently irresolute.

CHAPTER NINE

At four o'clock in the afternoon, when the watch was changed, the first lieutenant looked in on Hardinge. Seeing his captain asleep he frowned, shut the door quietly and went back on deck. It was most unfortunate – most unfortunate. He was shocked to realize how inadequate he felt; the ship had grown so big, and decisions so hard to make.

Now, in the dog watches a number of men were gathered on the fo'c'sle head. They leant companionably against the forward rail and while they talked their eyes were fixed on the frigate ahead. The retreating frigate? Or the one who led the race? The British sailors were more disposed to consider her the former.

'Will we catch that *Piemontaise*?' Beer asked.

'Sure we'll catch her. The old *San F.*'s the fastest frigate on the coast. The Frogs build 'em fast,' Lancarrow answered him.

'By all accounts you couldn't catch 'er last August,' Beer said.

'We was leaking twenty-four inches every watch, and our copper filthy an' ripped to glory. Now we's been docked, we'll overhaul her easy. Her bottom's foul if you like; not that we've seen much of it, 'cos she's been to windward all the time.'

"Twas you as took the *Psyché*, weren't it?'

'Yea. She was almost a sister-ship to us – smaller than that bastard ahead. Eh, but that were a fight, that were. Tho' we had a full crew aboard then –

ot like it is now with cooks an' stewards, waisters an'
ll sorts, a-manning of the guns.'

'The *Piemontaise*'ll be a good ship.'

'She be nowt but a bloody pirate, wi' a first loot-
nant that the admiral's made a fit subject for venge-
nce.'

'Why 'im 'specially?'

"Cos he spitted three o' the officers of the *Warren
Hastings* after she'd struck her flag. Tell you what,
chums, I'd be only too happy to take a dig at the bastard
myself – that I would.'

The fever was leaving the captain's body, and like
a swimmer nearing the shore he could already anticipate release from his ordeal. 'For lack of a frigate . . .'
A smile curled the corners of his lips. '. . . an island was
ost.' He'd damned well see the French did lose their
precious frigate!

Feeling horribly sick, he swung his legs from the
cot where he'd lain for four hours and staggered to
the door of his day cabin. The sun was sinking. The
gold light that flooded diagonally across the stern
windows laid a bright finger on the seat of the transom. Calling for King's help he changed his clothes,
and then, moving slowly, made his way up the ladder.

All the officers were on deck. He was aware of the
group at the same time as his eyes searched the sea
ahead. With delight he saw that the enemy was much
closer than he had dared hope. Dawson, the first to notice
his captain's presence, crossed to him as he stood holding on to the companionway.

'We're dong very nicely, Mr Dawson.' Hardinge
made no attempt to keep the usual reserve in his voice.

'Yes, indeed, sir. She's only a bare four miles ahead.
I did come down to tell you at four o'clock, but you

were sleeping, sir.' Dawson had all the appearance
of a man who has had a load removed from his mind
and Hardinge guessed that his re-appearance on deck
had been a great relief to his second-in-command.

'You've re-arranged the gun-crews?'

'Yes, sir, and had the salt-boxes topped up with
fresh cartridge. We're two men short on each gun
now, and I've taken one from each of the carronades
I know it will be difficult for the three men left, but
better that than to have nine of the great guns short
of a further man.'

'When does Dunnovan hope to make the convoy?'

'He reckons they'll be in sight from the masthead
by daybreak tomorrow, sir; although we're doing better
now, I believe, than when he made his reckoning an
hour ago.'

'We'll overhaul the enemy during the night,' Hardinge
said. Then seeing inquiry in Dawson's eyes, he deliberately turned away: he had not yet made up his mind
what he would do about it when they did.

CHAPTER TEN

With the coming of night it seemed that the *San Fiorenzo*'s speed increased – an illusion born of the narrowing limits of sight. Except up the moonpath, there was nothing to see but the black water that gurgled alongside, and, because the moon was high, even its path did not extend far from the ship. Its main effect was on the canvas that towered above them. There it sponged away the shadows and set the sails in windy silhouette against the plush darkness of the sky.

Conditions were very bad for trailing a ship that was so far away, and so, soon after eight o'clock, the *San Fiorenzo* lost sight of her quarry.

Hardinge, a dark and upright shadow, had hooked himself by an arm to the weather mizzen rigging as though, just by standing there, he could will the wind to drive his ship up to the enemy. Dawson, who had been more scared of Hardinge's sickness than anything the *Piemontaise* had done to them, approached the captain. 'Will you not go down below, sir? There's nothing you can do on deck until we have him in sight again.'

'Damn it, Dawson,' the captain spoke without turning his head, 'I'm not a child.'

'I know, sir – but we'll need you badly when we do.'

With an effort Hardinge stifled the temptation to let his temper fly. He wanted only to be left alone with his thoughts. At that moment even King's expressed solicitude would have been unbearable. The relationship between a captain and his first lieutenant was, Hardinge thought, always a peculiar one. The captain's deputy in everything, the first lieutenant was an intimate necessarily kept at a distance. A separate part of himself that somehow could never quite be admitted to full membership. 'No,' he said. 'No.' And then with a short laugh to make amends, 'You'll have to put up with my worrying around the deck.'

King, seeing the dampness of the night air and learning from Dawson of the captain's refusal to go down to rest, took up his tarpaulin. Appearing suddenly beside Hardinge, he held open the coat ready for slipping on, and almost before the captain was aware of it his hands were within the arms. King, who had the perspicacity to realize that a word spoken might result in the coat being refused, held his tongue.

The tension had communicated itself to the officers. As on the night before they stood about in groups, but, on this night of indecision they sought reassurance in silent companionship. Happier than most, Dunnovan, with a job to do, fussed over the set of each sail in turn. With the master's mate of the watch and a small party of sailtrimmers, he went from brace to sheet and back again, taking here a pull and there checking away a little on a rope. As he worked his way aft Hardinge called to him.

'Mr Dunnovan, do you make the wind to be easing?'

'Yes, sir – an' drawing a little to the west o' north.'

'I thought as much. It will probably come more westerly as we close the land. How far from the coast of Ceylon d'you reckon we are?'

''Bout fifty mile, sir.'

'What's she making?'

'It's nigh on time for Tulloch to heave the log-ship, sir. I'll have him do it now.'

'Very good. Let me know what it is.'

'Aye aye, sir.'

Dunnovan reported a few minutes later. 'A fraction under six knots, sir. 'Tis right that the wind has eased. She were making nigh on a knot better than that an hour agone.'

Hardinge pursed his lips and his fingers beat restlessly on the varnished rail capping. Up to a point the reduction in the power of the wind should be an advantage, for in the lighter weather the disparity between the ships could be expected to show even more. But there was a very definite limit to what was allowable in this respect. To handle a frigate to best advantage he needed at least enough wind to give him five knots, for below that speed his ship could scarcely be expected to pass the wind's eye when tacking, and could only be turned to another tack by wearing ship. Then his opponent would know for certain which way both ships must turn, and one tactic by which he could surprise the enemy would be denied him.

The watch dragged on while look-outs, below and aloft, official and self-appointed, strained their eyes to probe the deceptive darkness of the moonlit night. The wind continued its slow shift to the west and became lighter and lighter. At a quarter before eleven o'clock the log had given a speed of five and a half knots, and an hour later a quarter of a knot less.

At ten minutes to midnight the boatswain's mate was piping the middle watchmen on deck, and five minutes later the first men were coming up the hatchway. A murmur of voices rose in the waist, a soughing sound of breath expelled, such as a hive of disturbed bees might make when a shadow falls across it. Then, the period of uncertainty over, the cry was raised, assured and infinitely stimulating. 'Sail ho!' 'Sail ho!' 'Sail ho!'

'Where – away?' A dozen, two dozen, many many voices asked the same vital question.

'Broad on the bloody beam – see 'er? – 'tain't easy in this light – there away.'

'We've beaten the bastard at sailin' – now let's finish 'im orf wi' the guns.'

'Stop that jabbering! What in the hell d'you think you are – monkeys? Stop it, I say!' The boatswain's voice was raised above the babble of eager men who, pouring up from below, were swelling the crowd along the rail.

Dawson's broad-shouldered form materialized beside the slimmer shape of his captain. 'Beat to quarters, sir?'

But Hardinge did not answer the question. He stood withdrawn into himself as he stared over the sea. The rays of the moon, sinking in the west, illuminated the towering pinnacle of sails that was his beautiful enemy.

'No.' His mouth was tight-lipped, as if the decision had been difficult indeed to make. 'No, Mr Dawson. Do not beat to quarters. I sail for the convoy.'

Hardinge had learnt his lesson the hard way. He'd not be decoyed into chasing a moonlit will o' the wisp when the moon would set within the hour. He'd get down to his convoy as fast as his ship could take him, and let them bait the trap he hoped to spring.

BOOK FOUR

THE THIRD DAY

CHAPTER ONE

In silhouette against the sinking moon, the British frigate had been reported to Epron some minutes before the French ship had been seen by those on the deck of the *San Fiorenzo*. Epron and Moreau, hastily called, stood side by side at the rail; and, separated by their authority from the crowd that lined the ship's side, contemplated their enemy with a mixture of anger and bewilderment.

'Has she seen us?' Epron asked.

'How should I know?'

The captain, surprised at the shortness of the answer, shifted his scrutiny to the man beside him without being able to discern any particular expression on a countenance whose eye-pockets showed only as shadows in a moon-washed face. Stifling his resentment and trying to obtain a sympathetic understanding of his dilemma, Epron tried again.

'I was considering whether we should beat to quarters. Just in case he tries another night action.'

'He could do so.' Moreau stroked the blue jowl of his chin.

'You are not much help, my friend.'

'I shall obey whatever you order.'

It was on the tip of the exasperated Epron's volatile tongue to tell his first lieutenant just what value he placed on his assistance – which at the moment was little enough. Although he was fully aware that when battle was joined he could rely implicitly on the man's staunch loyalty. 'Whether he has seen us or not he is holding his course.'

'Then it is probable that he has not seen us.' The flat tones of Moreau's voice managed to re-convey that he preferred guns to theories and that if only his early advice had been accepted matters would have taken a different course.

'If he has not, then we must make it more difficult for him to do so. I don't wish to risk another night action, and a four point alteration of course will soon take us away from him.'

'And lose us distance!'

'It will only be for a little while. The moon will set within an hour, and who knows on which bow we shall find the convoy? It could be that they've made better speed than le Paysan has reckoned. Then we'll sight them on the port bow and it will suit us to be a few miles farther to the eastward.'

'They may just as likely have sailed rather more slowly and then they'll be farther than ever to the west.'

'Really,' Epron thought, 'the man is utterly impossible tonight.'

When the captain had come on deck he had flung a cloak over his shoulders. Now he settled it firmly, and used the gesture to gather authority. 'Moreau,' he said, 'as far as the convoy is concerned let us leave it that it is a fifty-fifty chance on which bow we find them. For the problem which is immediate, have the drummer beat to quarters and tell the officer of the watch to steer south-east. If the British captain does not wish to fight, there will be no action – but, if he does so wish, we know for certain that we have not the speed to avoid him. It is necessary to prepare ourselves.'

Then, having watched his first lieutenant move away, Epron turned once more to the ink-black silhouette that slid, as remorselessly as their own shadow, across the shimmering carpet of the moonlit sea. His voice, drowned by the first staccato crash of the drum, was heard only by himself. 'I'd give half my prize money to know if he has seen us,' Epron said.

To make the step aside might appear to be a minor decision, but it was one that emphasized again the fugitive nature of the Frenchman's mission. It may have been good tactics, but when the moon had set and Epron felt safe enough from interference to resume his course for the convoy and to 'stand down' his men, he knew that this uneventful call in the night had been far from good for the morale of a crew he had trained for aggression.

By and large the French captain was again unable to snatch any more sleep from the night than his opponent. He endured an agony of suspense and had plenty of time in which to savour it. Lonely and pacing the deck, Epron thought that the British captain must be a man of very peculiar character. He had first risked a night action and then followed it by fighting a quite unnecessary duel from a weak position, but on both occasions had succeeded in repairing with astonishing speed the damage that his foolhardiness had earned.

What was it that Decaen's agent had reported? That the *San Fiorenzo* had a new captain. It could perhaps be that her new commander was a young man. There had been much in her rash actions to suggest so, and by the same reasoning her change of tactics on this night appeared to indicate an ability to learn both prudence as well as strategy – for he could not, try as he would, bring himself to believe that his ship had not been seen by the British. It was most unfortunate that this young hot-head with his experienced crew should be on his trail – for just at the moment he, Epron, was feeling his age.

CHAPTER TWO

Hardinge, gripped by an utter disregard for the normal frailties of the human body, remained on deck throughout the night of uncertain wind. Between four and six bells in the middle watch the *San Fiorenzo* had logged only three knots, but now, with the breeze more settled in its new quarter, she was moving faster again. The fleeting glimpse of his quarry in the moonlight was all that had been granted to him; the *Piemontaise* had been slightly abaft the beam, soon lost to sight, and seen no more.

Whether her disappearance was the result of the setting of the moon, or a deliberate withdrawal of the enemy to the eastward, he had not been able to determine, and it was unfortunate that she had never been seen so plainly that any small tell-tale alteration in the bracing of her yards could have been noticed. It could have been due to deterioration of the visibility, or the Frenchman could have decided to increase the distance between the ships. The British captain would like to have known the answer, because if the last were true it would seem to indicate a lack of confidence on the part of the enemy which might provide a clue to his future actions. Hardinge now perceived that there was more to this fighting game than fisticuffs, and that the attitude of mind of the combatants could well affect the determination with which their thrusts were made. Imagining himself on the deck of the *Piemontaise*, he realized how perturbed he would have been to see the *San Fiorenzo* recover the position she had lost. It must have been a sad blow to the Frenchman's self-assurance. The thought brought a smile to his lips – the first that had appeared there since that nearly disastrous action of the previous morning.

Whatever the reason for her disappearance, he would much rather she had stayed in sight, not only because he would then know just where she was, but for the effect on the morale of his own men. They had expected him to fling his ship once more against the enemy, and had been disappointed that he had not. Even Dawson had appeared to anticipate that. A sensitive captain was always aware of the temper of his men, and he knew that after their exertions of the two past engagements they would have willingly attacked and gone on attacking until their ship had been battered to pieces beneath them. With such reasoning he could sympathize, for it awoke an answering chord in his own nature. But his new-found grasp of the larger issues had imposed on him, and through him on his men, a new discipline : the discipline of withholding fire until the tactical position was in his favour. Now, with his increased weakness, restraint was more than ever necessary.

The tournament of wits was at least as important as the engagement with guns. Somehow, somewhere, he had to bring his powerful enemy to battle in such a way that he would hold not only the tactical but if possible the moral advantage as well. He had to trick the Frenchman into a false move, and for that he would have to wait; to follow her every move in the hope that sooner or later she would either give him an opening or become so enraged at his continual anticipation and frustration of her movements that she would turn angrily to rend her tormentor, and lay herself open to retribution.

Dawson, coming up to take the deck at four o'clock, found his captain where he had left him three hours before.

'No sign of him at all.' Harding anticipated the question.

'Won't you rest now, sir? It'll not be dawn for another two hours, and I can call you as soon as we sight either the merchantmen or the enemy.'

Hardinge stirred, easing limbs that were cramped with chill, inactivity and the weight of the heavy tarpaulin coat. The thought of relaxation in his cot was very pleasant and a great temptation; and now that his second-in-command was on deck, there was no valid reason why he should not do so.

'Very well, Number One. Call me if anything should change. In any event have me called half an hour before dawn.' He turned to move towards the companionway, and hesitated. 'And, Mr Dawson, have some chocolate for me when I come up. Tell King to make a bowl for you too.' Then, moving stiffly, he made his way below, to fling himself into his cot and to find instant oblivion. Not even the refreshingly cool sound of water being pumped over the deck, nor the swish of brooms, nor the pad-pad of bare feet disturbed his sleep.

CHAPTER THREE

The dawn of the third day was very different from that of the days before, for now all the ships were close enough to the land to find the sunrise masked by clouds. Grey daylight had come before the sun, which, hiding its face, hung back beneath the shade that cast an apocalyptic gloom along the eastern horizon.

But by six o'clock the light was strong enough to disclose all the actors to each other. There were the three Indiamen: *Charlton*, Captain George Wood; *Metcalfe*, Captain Mathew Isacke, and *Devonshire*, Captain James Murrey. There were the *Piemontaise*, French fifty-gun frigate, and the British *San Fiorenzo* of thirty-eight guns: the one with a swollen company of over five hundred and twenty men, and the other with a depleted crew which now numbered no more than a hundred and fifty-four.

First seen as insubstantial shadows, the growing light hardened the outlines of steepled sails and chunky hulls into recognizable silhouettes. Everything seemed the same as it had been on the Sunday before, even to the equal sides of the triangle. But one vital question had been resolved, and one circumstance had changed. Both captains knew which ship was now the faster and the wind had shifted from north to north-west.

The players, so suddenly presented to each other by the rising of night, were taken by surprise; for though both the *Piemontaise* and *San Fiorenzo* had hoped that

18

dawn would reveal the convoy to them, neither had the least idea where the other would be. And so, while the warships headed for the convoy, Epron and Moreau on their quarterdeck, and Hardinge and Dawson on theirs, had the problem to discuss.

'What will you do?' Moreau asked of Epron.

Epron began the pacing back and forth that Moreau knew so well. 'I do not know. I do not know. *Sacré nom!* He has the luck of the devil. For us, he is in just the worst position possible. If we stand on for the convoy it is certain that he will intercept us. If we haul our wind on the port tack we shall . . . *Sacré nom!*' It seemed that such exasperation could even dry up the fountain of Epron's speech.

'If you alter to port, you'll run on the coast of Ceylon,' Moreau reminded his captain.

'Do you think I do not know that?' The shorter man paused in his pacing and spun round.

'Then if you want the convoy, you must fight him.'

'My friend, do not forget that the convoy will sail again from Ceylon in two or three days' time. We can intercept it then – it will be larger by the ships from Calcutta and Madras.'

'If the *Sémillante* has not already taken one or two, or even all in prize,' Moreau goaded his superior.

'The *Sémillante*. Bah!' Epron winced as the thrust went home, 'What has that *cavalière servante*, Motard, ever done? A few small country ships! Nothing. Nothing at all. To be brave it is not necessary to be fool-hardy.'

'And yet, captain, he will fight you if he wishes, whether you will or no, for if you bring her on the wind on the starboard tack he is so far to windward as to be certain to weather us. Captain Epron, you have the more powerful ship. Let us run down for the convoy.'

'But that is obviously what he wants me to do!'

'What do you make of him now, Mr Dawson?' It was Hardinge speaking.

'I reckon we hold him in a most awkward position, sir.' Dawson's voice was warm with anticipation.

'I agree. I think he's between the devil and the deep.'

'Between the *San F.* and the beach?'

'That's just about it,' Hardinge agreed. 'You see, Dawson, he's got to make up his mind now. If he were to try the starboard tack he'd still have to fight us just the same, and he'd be going away from the convoy. Even if we were to be beaten, we'd almost certainly wound him so much that he'd be in no shape at all to catch the merchantmen before they make Colombo.'

'Somehow, sir, I don't reckon he'll have a bite at the convoy – not with us around. We hit him pretty hard yesterday.'

'You know, Dawson, if I were he, I'd take a chance and brace up on the port tack. It would put him six miles ahead of us and it would take us at least six hours to catch him. Anything could happen in that time. The wind could come more westerly – anyway it probably will as we close the land. Then in this northerly weather there's often a strong southerly set near the coast, and he might get into that a long time before we did. He'd maybe catch the convoy more easily by making a big half circle to the eastward.'

Epron was calling. 'Where is Monsieur le Paysan? Le Paysan!' And when the master had detached himself from the knot of officers that hung about the lee rail and hurried to him, 'Le Paysan, is there not a strong current down the coast?'

'Sometimes, yes. In the season of northerly winds it can run at as much as two knots.'

'You agree that the local wind will come more westerly as we near the land?'

'Without a doubt.'

'Then, Moreau, let us come on the wind on the port tack. We may still arrive at the convoy before our friend.'

'We shall be very close to Colombo,' Moreau grumbled.

'That does not matter. Out of gunshot of the fort is as good as twenty leagues at sea. Besides it will be fun to have the British colony spectators of the action.'

'I do not like it, Captain Epron. We should fight our way to the convoy now.'

'You are a fool, Moreau – a fool. We are more than a thousand miles from Port Louis. Monsieur le Paysan, brace round the yards. Laporte, put your helm down – steer east.'

'His stu'n'sail sheets have been started, sir.' Dawson spoke out of the side of his mouth as he kept his glass trained on the enemy frigate.

'Mr Dawson, have the watch stand by,' Hardinge answered as he raised his own glass. 'He's swinging his mainyard now. He's altering to port. Newington, put your helm down, let her head come up to east.'

'Aye aye, sir. Steer east, sir.'

The chase was on again – but the *Piemontaise*, nearly six miles ahead, was sailing a course that would apparently take her farther and farther away from the convoy. Hardinge understood the reason for her doing so, and could only hope that his faster ship would enable him to bring the enemy to action.

And he could well imagine with what relief the merchant captains, who must have viewed the repetition of the setting of two days before with some anxiety, would see the notorious enemy altering away from them, with the British frigate again in hot pursuit.

CHAPTER FOUR

The clouds above the island did not disperse, but hung about all morning on the mountains, and even extended seaward to cover a large portion of the adjoining ocean. Beneath this tenuous canopy the wind became coy and fitful, blew from any point between north and west, and from no particular one for any length of time. Nor did either ship experience the southerly drift, for this was more dependent on the direction of the wind in the Gulf of Oman, and the extreme north of the Arabian Sea, than it was affected by the local breeze.

By noon, after a morning of constant sail-trimming in both ships, and of extreme vexation to all concerned, it was obvious that whatever the outcome of any engagement between the frigates, the convoy itself would certainly make Colombo without interference. Thus far the *San Fiorenzo*, by her presence and by her persistence, had secured her main object – the safe and timely arrival of the convoy. The knowledge that she had done so was as much a tonic to the tired Hardinge as it was an added vexation to the equally exhausted Epron, who now saw his plan defeated by lack of wind, and his judgement once again proved at fault before Moreau.

But even worse was the fact that he was obviously going to be brought to action by a ship which, though she might be much weaker than his own, would almost certainly deal him many fresh wounds, and when finally taken be worth only a fraction of the price which any one of the Indiamen would have brought. As each hour brought the faster sailing *San Fiorenzo* nearer to her enemy, her ship's company became more jubilant as surely as the crew of the *Piemontaise* grew more sullen and morose.

Slowly but surely, in the fickle winds, the British worked their ship up to, and dead astern of, the French vessel. Running in the same grain as the enemy, Hardinge was then able to choose whichever side best suited him whenever the *Piemontaise* turned at bay; and, with the hills of Ceylon already visible amongst the clouds ahead, turn she must.

At noon the French frigate had led the British by three miles, and the coast had been some sixteen miles ahead. By half past one only a mile and a half separated the ships, with land ten miles distant from the *San Fiorenzo.*

It was Dunnovan, on whose face the lines of tiredness and strain were deeply etched, who first noticed the cloud movement. 'D'you see the way the clouds are shifting over the hills, sir? Drifting to the south'ard all the time, an' seemingly getting less heavy. Reckon the wind'll veer smartly to the norrard, sir.'

For some minutes Hardinge watched the phenomenon. Then slowly he nodded his head. 'You're right. I've seen just the same thing off the Andalausian coast – the clouds on the mountain flanks moving before the surface wind shifts. We'll work out to the north of her. Burn!' He turned to call to the quartermaster, 'Let her come up half a point.'

'Aye aye, sir.' The long jib-boom moved across the horizon to port, and the *Piemontaise* then appeared on the starboard bow : 'Course, east a half north, it is, sir.'

All the officers and nearly all the ship's company were on deck, for there were very few who could live alone with their impatience. Dawson moved expectantly nearer to his captain. 'Yes please, Mr Dawson, you may beat to quarters. We'd best be ready. He can't put off the inevitable much longer.'

'Sir, the enemy's taking in his stu'n'sails,' Davies, the officer of the watch, reported.

'Then we may do the same. Mr Dunnovan, I'll have the stu'n'sails off her, please. Smartly as you can, for I'd not like him to know how short-handed we are. You may take the full watch from the guns. He can't surprise us now.'

In the sunless sweltering heat the yards were manned. One by one, starting at the t'gallants, the men on each mast set down the stu'n'sails, relieving the ship of sails that could only be a hindrance in battle. So might a man, taking off an unwieldy coat, prepare himself for the fray.

Half an hour dragged by. Then suddenly excitement rose, for all along the northerly horizon the sky showed blue, as, down from the north, came the true wind. First seen as a surprisingly dark line between sea and sky, the band of wind-ruffled water grew lighter in colour as it neared the ships, but remained surprisingly blue. Both frigates had braced their yards to meet the expected wind. Ahead of them the sunlight pierced the clouds and placed golden fingers upon the green forest that mantled the hills. The lightening in the weather revived the heart-warming creak of masts and spars, the talk of sheaves in the blocks, the sibilant grinding of wind-tautened ropes, the listing of the ship, and a chuckle of water moving ever faster along her side.

'A grand start to the action, Mr Dawson. If this

wind holds, and it surely will, we'll have a fine breeze with which to handle her. The old *San F.* can still sail like a witch – she always could so long as her bottom was clean. I remember when Captain Tyler and I took her home after we salvaged her in 'ninety-four. We picked up a sou'wester off Lisbon and logged more than twelve knots for twenty-four hours – anchored off the Hamoaze five days out from Gibraltar. So long as we can keep sailing, he'll have no chance to board and make use of all those men. We'll start with the weather gauge this time and keep it. We'll stay away from him and shoot him up until he strikes. And, Mr Dawson, pass the word for Mr Moysey and for the gunner and his mates; I'd talk with them, and like you to be present when I do.'

Moysey, the gunnery officer, Bird and his four gunner's mates, were soon gathered round Hardinge and Dawson at the base of the mizzen mast, and waited confidently for the captain to speak.

'When he comes at us,' the captain explained, 'we'll pass on opposite tacks – he to leeward on the starboard tack, while we are on the port. I don't want each gunlayer to fire his gun as soon as the sights will bear, but to fire a controlled broadside together. The range will be very short – I'll see to that. The effect of all our shot arriving at the same time will be doubly discomforting for him: it'll be a discipline I don't think he could achieve and will greatly affect his morale. It means complete control at the guns. You'll take your time from Mr Moysey in the waist ...'

'Enemy's tricing up his mainsail, and has dropped his jib, sir.'

All eyes looked over the starboard bow. A mile away, the Frenchman lay over to the now fresh breeze.

'He's hauling over his spanker boom, sir.'

'His foretack's raised, sir.'

'He's tacking, sir!'

Hardinge's eyes shone with the excitement of battle. 'Get to your stations,' he said to the group around him. 'Run out your guns!'

CHAPTER FIVE

The Frenchman had completed his turn. The two frigates approached each other on opposite tacks, and there was nothing Epron could do to save his passing to leeward of the *San Fiorenzo*. The Britisher had earned the weather gauge, and only further injury to her spars could wrest it from her.

Like knights in joust the ships moved together. Each steered to pass close by the other, and, white-mantled under their sails, the two pinnacles of canvas were inclined the same way. And if the ships relied for victory on the corporate endeavour of their crews, these were as much enclosed within their wooden shells as ever the knightly challengers had been within their armour.

It was easier for the men of the *San Fiorenzo* to understand for what they fought than it could be for those in the *Piemontaise*. If they fought for themselves, they fought also for King George and for all those who hated tyranny whether they were squires in the manor houses or cowmen in the byres. The *Piemontaise* as surely represented her own nation, and its Republic that had proclaimed *liberté, égalité, fraternité*. But for French thought to adventure far on to such ground was to find itself in a morass as dangerous as any their cavalry had encountered at Agincourt. The Republic which had dethroned a king had given birth to an emperor. The age-old aristocracy had been torn down, to reveal – what? A new one made of generals, marshals and petty kings.

What for days Hardinge had thought of as a slow overhauling had now become a rushing together. To discover if she were nearer there was no longer need for Dunnovan to take sextant angles of the enemy's masthead. As each moment passed the details of the enemy spars and hull could be seen more plainly. There were the wounds made by their guns in that first night's encounter that seemed so long ago. The run of each rope could be followed with ease. The heads of men could be seen as her crew stood to the line of carronades on the upper deck. A man scampered aloft to clear some piece of rigging that had fouled, and the white crossbelts of the blue-coated musketeers in her tops were plainly visible. Nearer and nearer she came, until she filled the bulk of the horizon; until the head must be tilted to glance up at her swaying masthead with the long blue-white-blue man o' war pennant. The sea beneath her black bows was creaming white. The two rows of open ports showed dark with the menace of her guns. Her sails were arched and beautifully trimmed. The long jib-boom, its jib down in hanks and bunched like a nosegay at the outer end, was almost level with their own.

Fifty yards now separated the rushing hulls. Lanyards in hand, the gun-captains knelt behind their guns with left hands raised to tell the gunnery officer that their piece was ready to fire.

A round blob of cotton wool appeared from the foremost of the enemy's guns, and was whipped backwards across the French hull by the now fresh wind. It was followed by another and another as the ripple of fire passed down the enemy's flank. Hardinge could see the knot of officers gathered on her quarter-deck – blue laced with gold under the black wings of their cocked hats. A ball whined over his head.

A shroud parted with the twang of a slack violin string loosely plucked. A shot hit somewhere with a plunk – the sound of a man chopping wood in a garden.

Another noise of a hit was followed by the high-pitched sound of a whip. 'He's firing grape, sir,' Dawson said of the metal frames which, embracing eighteen two-pound shot, would burst on hitting to send the balls in all directions.

Hardinge glanced at Moysey. The gunnery officer stood hat in hand upon a salt-box the better to view the enemy. The captain knew a long second of anxiety, for fear the officer should delay too long. The hat fell. A second later the *San Fiorenzo*'s nineteen gun broadside fired – not quite as one, but, even more threatening, like a roll of thunder. Beneath her men's feet the ship shuddered to the concussion of the discharge. The gun-wheels rumbled on the seamed deck. The wind blowing through the cloud of smoke dispersed it instantly to leeward. A number of scars showed on the flank and on the bilge of the enemy as it was carried clear of the waves by the angle at which she sailed.

The first assay was over.

'Stop your vents. Sponge your guns.'

'Prepare to load.'

The guns' crews flung themselves upon their charges. Every now and then trickles of blue smoke emerged from the muzzles, where fragments of the canvas powder bags still smouldered.

'Most satisfactory, I think, Mr Dawson; we could hardly have hoped to hit him more fairly.'

'I reckon when he comes about on the other tack, he'll discover himself to be leaking.'

'As soon as ever the wads have been rammed down, you'd best call away the port watch to tack the ship.'

'Aye aye, sir. Boatswain's mate, pipe, Port watch to tack ship.'

The two contestants, reaching the end of the mile-long lists, were upright in the sea. Their sails flogged as they tacked in unison. Together their bows fell off towards each other. They heeled, gathered speed, hauled aft their sheets and swept against each other.

'Make ready for action on the other side.' The order was given as soon as it was sure that once more they would weather the enemy.

Hastily the men at the guns, who were being rejoined by those taken away to handle the ship, secured the guns on the starboard side. Fastening aprons over the vents, hanging the priming horns and tube boxes on the cascables, they hurried across to prepare the port side guns for action.

Once the ships had pointed towards each other, little more than three minutes would elapse before they met. The Frenchman, with lascars to handle his sails while his men had only to fight their guns, should have been better placed than the Britisher, but the *Piemontaise* had proved to be no faster in stays than the *San Fiorenzo*. And even as the ships came together again Hardinge noticed that the luff of the Frenchman's fore topsail was badly set.

'She doesn't look so happy as she did last time,' the captain said to Dawson.

'Indeed she doesn't, sir – and look at her side!'

It was the first time since her own mainyard had been shot down the day before that they had clearly seen the port side of their enemy when it was not hidden by the smoke of both ships' guns.

The long jib-booms were overlapping. The bows passed. The sun shone on both ships alike. Tense men waited, oblivious for the moment of sun, wind and sea, and eager only to see their weapons fired.

The enemy's forward guns were firing, then those amidships. A shot passing low across the waist wounded the tackle of the main brace on the weather side. It was not under stress, but they would need it, and need it badly, when next day they tacked ship. Dawson ran forward towards the barricade. The master and Tulloch were already there. It was not strictly Dunnovan's job as master to work with his own hands, but they were so desperately short of men that rank must be forgotten.

More shots passing, hitting. Grape whined in the air. Their own guns thundered. A small frightened face appeared beside Dawson's arm. 'What is it, boy?' For a moment Dawson was surprised that such a steady lad should show such fear. A ball hit the muzzle of one of the after carronades and went screaming past them. Marsingal did not flinch, so it could not be fear for himself. Doubtless it was some message from the captain. Dawson bent his head. 'What is it, boy?' he asked again.

'The captain, sir,' Marsingal stammered. 'He's fallen, sir.'

CHAPTER SIX

Hardinge, wounded by a grape shot between shoulder and breastbone, had been carried below. Dawson, second-in-command, was left for the first time without the shield that he had made of the captains he had served, and now the decisions of Olympus were his alone to make – and without time to think.

The *San Fiorenzo* took a sheer to port.

'Watch your steering there, Newington.' The words carried a new found emphasis. Used to speak under the patronage of another, Dawson was now the sole authority. It was, he discovered, just as easy without a captain beside him. Like a man who can swim, but cannot dive, he was being forced by the inexorable – the built-up reputation of the *San Fiorenzo* and the will of her men – to take the plunge. Glancing astern, he could see the Frenchman still going away, but she would surely be tacking soon.

'Boats'n's mate. Pipe, Port watch tack ship.'

Dunnovan, the brace spliced, was back on the quarterdeck, approaching him, waiting for orders. Young Marsingal, like a dog who had lost his owner, hung round hopeful of recognition.

'Here boy, keep handy so I can call you if I need you.'

The midshipman hurried to him gratefully.

'Haul over the boom.'

It was as simple as that. The whole intricate business was working just as well for him as for . . . as for . . . Oh well, time enough to worry when they'd beaten the Frenchman. And he'd been frightened of this for years. When they'd fought the *Psyché* and his Captain Lambert had . . .

'Helm a-lee – raise tacks and sheets.'

. . . when Captain Lambert had insisted on standing a-top a carronade so that he could better see the enemy he had been scared. Not scared of the enemy or frightened for Lambert, but frightened for himself . . .

'Mainsail haul.'

. . . because if anything had happened to Lambert he'd have had to do just this – and that had been three years ago.

The ship was spinning round. She really was a delight to handle. Through his feet, flat on the deck, she was telling him what she wanted her captain – her acting captain – to do.

'Haul taut weather braces. Haul the bowlines.'

Dawson breathed a deep sigh of satisfaction and turned his eyes from his own ship to the Frenchman.

'Captain, sir – er – Mr Dawson, sir.' Dawson turned to find Davies at his side. 'The enemy's missed stays. She's tried to make a stern board but fallen back on the same tack.'

'Those lascars like as not. I'd not like to take a hammering like the last we gave him – not with all those coloured boys aboard.'

'He's brailing up his foresail and spanker, sir. He's waiting for us.' Davies had his glass raised again.

'It's an assignation I'll be delighted to keep.'

Funny, Dawson thought, he was even saying the sort of things that captains were expected to say – phrases he'd never thought he could turn. Perhaps it was because he'd heard so many captains talk. Perhaps the ability to do so was passed on by one to another – on and on and would never stop. The mantle of the old falling on the shoulders of the new.

'Quartermaster. Let her fall off a point. Keep him fine on the port bow.'

'Aye aye, sir. Steer west by south, sir. Keep 'im fine on the bow, sir.' Newington, feet braced, eased the wheel over a spoke or two.

'Make ready for action on the other side.'

CHAPTER SEVEN

'Moreau! Le Paysan! Moreau!' Epron called, and
then to the ensign beside him, 'Quick, quick. Fetch
me Monsieur Moreau or the master.' Then, catching
sight of his first lieutenant already taking from the
guns enough men to handle the ship, the captain
called the boy back. 'Ensign, Ensign – come back to me.
Do not disturb the officers from their work.'

Epron was appalled: not by the violence of the
enemy's fire, but by the behaviour of the natives.
The last broadside had made them run in terror from
the deck to hide below in any nook or cranny they could
find.

The master's mates were gathering to their parties
the men sent to them. Epron, glancing at the enemy,
saw that his own ship should now be turning.

'Raise tacks and sheets. Haul over the spanker.
Quick. Quick. Gailteux, put your helm a-lee.' In
his haste, preparatory orders were overlooked, and
anyway, now that the decks had been cleared of the
riff-raff that Decaen had put aboard, the ship seemed
wholly French again. His own sailors would understand. Orders could be cut short. Epron's spirits rose.

'Mainsail haul. Off all haul.'

The *Piemontaise* was turning: coming up into the
wind. Experienced hands hauled the braces. The mainyard began its swing. The maintopsail followed obedi-
ently and the yards above it on the main. But those
on the foremast were slow to swing – too slow. Epron,
from aft, saw men running: saw Moreau's arm des-

perately waving above the crowd as he gave directions the captain could not hear. Something had gone wrong in an exactly timed manoeuvre that allowed no latitude – no latitude at all. Le Paysan ran past him going forward.

The captain again looked over his shoulder at the British frigate. She too had begun her turn and even then hung in the wind's eye. His jealous eye saw her foresail belly and fill on the new tack as her foremast yards swung round. Her tacks were being settled. She was round, and his ship – his own much loved *Piemontaise* – was caught in stays with her foresail, for some reason, held a-back.

An ensign came running from forward. 'Captain. The fore-brace was wounded by a shot. It parted when they hauled . . .'

'Gailteux. Reverse your helm. Quickly, quickly.' Epron ran to the ship's side. The *Piemontaise* barely moved through the water. The waves slip-slopped lazily along her flank. The backed foresail had stopped her way – was pressing her astern. Even now with the rudder reversed there was a chance, a slim one, that by allowing her to make a sternboard he might yet cause her head to fall off in the direction of the enemy.

The captain's eyes anxiously followed the jib-boom to watch which way it would creep across the horizon. For long seconds it moved not at all. A moment of doubt was followed by the horror of certainty. The ship was falling back on the same tack from which she had started – with no time to gather way and try again before her enemy would be upon her. It would be far too dangerous to be caught in stays by such a hard-hitting opponent. There was nothing for it but to wait on this, the starboard tack, until his enemy should close on him. Epron was now forced to fight from exactly the same position, and under the same disadvantage, as that from which the British captain had chosen to start the previous day's engagement. As the Englishman had done, the Frenchman brailed up his foresail and spanker, and, watching his enemy's approach, saw the *San Fiorenzo*'s fore tack and sheet climb from the deck, her spanker brailed up to the gaff, and her fore t'gallant staysail slide down the stay. The Britisher had been quick to appreciate the position and to pick up the fresh gauntlet that Epron had flung down.

If one of the jousting pair had been, as it were, unhorsed, it was not the end of the matter. There were other methods of fighting, and Epron still had confidence in his own fine frigate; perhaps even more now that action had purged the lascars from her decks.

To Epron it now seemed certain that this unfortunate meeting would result in his receiving so much damage that he would have to give up his cruise and return to Port Louis—but at least he would take the Britisher along with him in prize. Although not worth very much in herself, her removal from the coast would make matters that much easier for the *Sémillante*. And his compatriot frigate should be reaching her cruising ground off the south coast of Ceylon any time within the next fortnight. If his own pocket was not likely to be enriched very much, the outcome of this fight could be of benefit to others.

CHAPTER EIGHT

In the dim cockpit, down on the platform below the after end of the berth deck, and lit only by candles in their lanthorns, the sounds of battle were rarified.

Ward bent over the injured captain. One glance was sufficient. In a quiet room ashore and in a temperate climate he could have tried, however unsuccessfully, to mend the appalling damage. But Ward was only an ordinary ship's surgeon, not a magician, and there was nothing he could do. He drew the rough blanket over the gaping hole and knelt beside his friend.

Hardinge, who had virtually lost consciousness on the agonizing journey down, returned to mental awareness of his position. A numbness claimed his body, as if the hurt were too mortal to register pain, and though he could hardly see, his brain was uncommonly clear and entirely concerned for his ship. How would Dawson fare now that command had fallen to him? Would his own carefully thought out plan be allowed to disintegrate into one of those dog-fights where both sides blazed away at each other until exhaustion forced the weaker to strike? They were so desperately weak that such a course could have only one end.

His ears and sense of balance desperately probed the dark, and brought him almost as much knowledge as if he had been on deck. The guns were still firing slow organized broadsides. The ship rocked and quivered to their discharge. Dawson had not let up.

Then for a while, although French shot could still

be heard crashing against the port side, the guns of his own ship fell silent. He knew from the feel of the deck beneath him that she was moving slowly to the south-west and guessed that she had fore-reached on her opponent. Almost as an answer to his thought came the pipe. 'Port watch to wear ship.' Hardinge guessed the reason that had called forth the order. Dawson was going to cross the Frenchman's bows, and then, hauling his wind on the port tack, engage her lee side at point blank range. The need for the enemy to change his men from one broadside to the other would help to offset any disadvantage of the temporarily assumed lee berth, while damage done to the shrouds that held the French masts on the starboard side would be doubly severe if those on her port side could also be hurt. Dawson, he thought, must be very sure of himself to undertake such a manoeuvre, but it was the plan they had discussed together.

The ship was turning now. He could feel her pitch, pause, and be carried forward again as the waves came up from astern. 'Hands working ship to your quarters.' Hardinge smiled and a trickle of blood escaped his lips Ward wiped it away with a cloth.

'Double shot your guns.'

That was good.

'Double shot your carronades – one round ball, one round grape.'

That was better and better. Dawson was going to sweep by and blast the Frog to glory. What a pity the battle was being fought in the gentle wind of the Indian Ocean and not in the bright hard weather of the Atlantic, where a ship could really be sailed and her men catch exhilaration from her own swift movements.

The Frenchman was firing, the boom of the guns

crept irregularly into the cockpit where Hardinge lay.
He could hear the tearing crash of metal on wood —
and still no reply from his own guns. The *San Fiorenzo*
shivered under the blows. Men cried out, and quick
footsteps ran along the deck above his head. Damage
had been done, how much he did not know. Then
at last it came. Like a rat shaken by a terrier, the old
frigate shivered. Her oak beams screamed above the
thunderous discharge of her double-shotted guns whose
recoil was so much greater than when only a single
round was fired.

For a breathless moment there was silence, and then,
as the smoke cleared away, a cheer went up. Started
away forward on the fo'c'sle by those who had first
been able to see past the cloud, it spread like a flame
through the ship, lifting men's hearts.

'Ward — Ward — find out . . .' Hardinge murmured.

The surgeon rose and ran from the narrow place
with its stench of blood and death. After the cheering,
a silence settled over the ship : the taut silence of
men who watch events is doubly tantalizing for those
who may not see. Ward was not long gone. As he
knelt again, Hardinge saw in the light of the lanthorns
that his eyes were wide with delight.

'God ! I've never seen such a mess, sir. Her main
and mizzen have gone — less than a couple of fathoms
above the deck — everything's down above the fore
top, and the fore mast itself swaying from side to side.
All that's down is hanging over his port side, masking
his guns. They daren't fire a shot on that side until
they've cut away the wrack, or they'll set her on fire.'

'Port watch tack ship.' The boatswain's call was
faintly heard.

So Dawson was going to sail round and round her.
With her masts gone it could only be a question of

time. Time? Time for him to go? He didn't wan
to go. Not yet. There was so much he wanted from
life. So much he'd not yet tasted. Women. He'd neve
found time to make the effort. He'd thought he coul
leave all that until he'd fought his way to the to;
and could take his pick. But now he'd never eve
captain a ship of the line.

'Ward.' His voice was stronger.

'Sir?'

'My compliments to Mr Dawson, and tell him—
tell him – well done you !'

'Aye aye, sir.' Ward made to rise but a change i
his patient's face brought him to his knees again. H
bent his ear until it almost brushed the pale lips.

'Ward.'

'Sir?'

'Change that message. My compliments to Captai
Dawson.'

CHAPTER NINE

With the fall of his masts, Epron felt that his honour and all he hoped from life had crashed with them into the sea. To be beaten was bad: to be thrashed by a ship so much weaker insupportable. Where for so many years his masts had held above him the towered tracery of spars and cordage, there was nothing. He stood alone under the bare sky, and knew the next move that he must make.

But there was no tricolour left to haul down. His ship, a dismasted hulk, had not one spar left above deck level.

Slowly, heavily, he set himself to climb upon the tumbled wrack that had been the spanker boom and sail. He would wave to the British – they would understand that.

Moreau had seized an axe and with a party of sailors was attempting to hack away the clutter of spars, cordage and canvas that hung over the port side. It was not until the captain had reached the top of the spar that the first lieutenant noticed him. Realizing what Epron intended, Moreau began to gesticulate and shout: 'Epron! Epron! You are not to surrender! Epron!'

But the captain, if indeed he heard, took no notice.

Moreau drew his pistol and levelled it carefully at the captain.

A sailor, horror in his face, struck up the first lieutenant's arm.

For a moment Moreau, standing on the gunwale,

DIAGRAM TO EXPLAIN TUESDAY'S ACTION

WIND

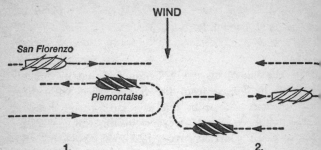

1.
Epron, driven beyond endurance, and with the land close ahead, turns at bay to meet Hardinge's threat.

2.
Both ships 'tack' after the first engagement.

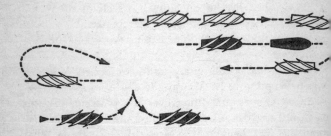

3.
After the second exchange the *San Fiorenzo* tacks successfully, but the *Piemontaise* 'misses stays' and falls back on the same tack. Epron then decides to wait for his adversary to come down to him.

4.
The Piemontaise receives the worst of the gun battle. The *San Fiorenzo* crosses her bows and attacks the uninjured side bringing down all three masts.

ooked at the man. But his eyes were focused far beyond and held no recognition of any individual.

'You fool!' he hissed. Then he turned the pistol to his own breast and pressed the trigger.

The body slumped and fell outboard. It rolled slowly down the swath of sail that had once been the main topsail, hung for a moment in the water-logged canvas at the foot, and was at last received by the waves.

'Cor – take a look at that!' Lancarrow said. 'The silly bastard's shot 'isself! Damned excitable chaps they be, foreigners,' and he spat with precision through the port into the sea.

'What did he want to do that for?' Beer asked.

"Cos it were Moreau for certain sure. He weren't going to wait for no admiral's vengeance. His sins 'as caught him up, that's all.'

'What do you reckon the *Piemontaise* be worth in prize money?'

'Who can say? Depends if they buys her into the Service. I suppose ten thousand or so – but then the prize agent has his cut, and by the time it comes down to the likes of you and me I doubt we'll get twenty pound apiece. Still with all those men aboard – and cor, aren't they thick upon her deck? – the head money will add up to a tidy sum. And so, d'you see, lads, it were worth that work at the pumps! Reckon I c'ld do twenty-four hours without a spell, so be as I could watch three masts shot through again and see 'em sent a-skittling overside.' The experienced seaman could put the action and the gale in correct perspective.

The crew of number one gun had been clustered round the port. They were recalled to their duties by the boatswain's mates, who were piping round the ship: 'Sailtrimmers to back maintopsail,' and again, 'A-way

launch — a-way launch. All hands on deck. Hoist out
the launch.'

On the quarterdeck Surgeon Ward approached Dawson
with the list of casualties. He moved slowly, knowing
that he was about to confirm news already supposed to
be bad.

'The captain?' Dawson queried as soon as Ward
was near enough for his question, couched in con-
fidential tones, to be heard.

The surgeon, turning down the corners of his mouth,
shook his head. 'That message to you was the last thing
he said.'

'He knew then?'

'He knew all the time. We both knew.'

'Yes,' Dawson said. 'I saw him carried below. We
all knew.' For a moment both men stood looking out
across the narrow band of water that separated the
ships. 'At least you were able to tell him about that.
It must've helped.'

'It was all he wanted. His whole soul was set on that
these last three days.'

'He was a good man, and a good captain. They usu-
ally go together — but not always. I've lost a friend.'
Dawson spoke slowly and with hesitation as he groped
for words to clothe thoughts which of themselves appeared so naked. 'I'd feel more grief if I thought he'd
left more behind. He always gave me the impression that
he had a great deal to die for, but not much to live for.'

'He was wrong there. I know one thinks that way
sometimes — but it must be wrong.'

'Maybe it is, but that sort of thought is just as true
as we think it is. I'm no hand at explaining, but I'm
sure he believed he was being honest with himself.
You couldn't have a man who was more so.'

Davies, who had just seen the launch put in the water, joined the two officers. Dawson returned his salute and asked, 'Mr Ward, what of the other casualties?'

'Besides the captain, two seamen and one marine dead, sir. Lieutenant Moysey's badly hurt, but I think he'll live. Five seamen wounded – Pope's very bad, sir – and two marines.'

'Another twelve men! A hundred and thirty-six men left. Not much more than half our proper complement, and God alone knows how many there are in the Frenchman. More than five hundred for sure. Mr Davies, I'll send fifty men over with you in the launch – it will mean two trips – and you'd best send some of the Frenchmen back aboard here – anything up to a hundred. I'll take the prize in tow as soon as you're ready.'

Ward had gone down to the cockpit to look after his patients. Davies had returned to the waist to see to the loading of the launch with the first party of the prize crew. Midshipman Lefroy, who was to accompany the lieutenant into the *Piemontaise*, and Marsingal, who was to bring the boat back for the second party, were already in the launch that rode alongside. Dunnovan and his mates were repairing the rigging and, when the most urgent necessities had been seen to, would have to make ready the big hawser for taking in tow the dismasted frigate.

For the moment Dawson was alone. The sun on his back was very pleasant. In this moment of respite the first lieutenant's eye lighted on the ship's cat: the cat that had, six years before, been brought aboard in Plymouth Sound, a kitten in the breast of a drunken sailor's pea-jacket. She paced delicately down the deck, and was careful to keep her immaculate toes from the sun-softened pitch in the seams. In search of quiet, and a patch of warmth after the din and disturbance of the last hour and a half, she stepped lightly on to the knee of the man who crouched on the carriage of the after carronade. A small pippin from which the juice of life seemed to have been drained, King sat with his eyes fixed steadfastly on the bright sea astern, which, calm and serene, was devoid of any sign of man's brutality to man.

APPENDIX

Although I have preferred to tell this tale as fiction rather than history, it must be remembered that it is a story of events that really happened : events which had their repercussions on men, on ships, and on the fortune of war in eastern waters. So for those who are interested, this footnote is added; and for the same reasons I have included diagrams descriptive of the action on the second and third day.

Despite their 'secret weapon' of the bomb, it was a thoroughly bad week for the French. Seven days after Epron had had to surrender the *Piemontaise*, Motard of the *Sémillante* was in trouble. He had succeeded in intercepting the Calcutta convoy escorted by the *Terpsichore*, whose captain Montague had in fact landed his upper deck carronades at Madras and so was greatly inferior to his opponent. But even with this disadvantage the British had no hesitation in attacking. In the course of the action the *Sémillante* was able to get close enough alongside to release one of her bombs, and, although it killed the crews of four of the midship guns it neither damaged the guns themselves nor stopped their being fired. For, with no carronades to man, spare crews were readily available. The explosion can hardly be said to have had the desired effect, for the use of what the British sailors considered a most inhuman weapon made them so mad with rage that in twenty minutes of fiercely fought action they beat off the Frenchman and so wounded her that she could never afterwards be used as a cruiser.

The *Piemontaise* was bought into the Royal Navy

and, after refitting, helped to take part in the final reduction of the Ile de France. The *San Fiorenzo*, twenty years older than her opponent, could not be repaired in India. She was patched up, and Dawson took her home. Given acting rank by Sir Edward Pellew on the latter's victorious return from Sourabaya, the Admiralty later confirmed Dawson's promotion to Post Captain. But even Greenwich Dockyard could not repair the wounds received by so old a ship. The *San Fiorenzo*, that had been launched in the year in which Hardinge was born, had been salvaged with the help of his own hands, never again fired a gun in action. Laid up in Stangate Creek, she served as a store ship until she was finally taken to pieces in 1837.